BLOSSOM

THE WONDERFUL ADVENTURES OF A RAINBOW LORIKEET

MICHAEL COLLINS

Adapted from
The Blossom and Buzz Musical Trilogy
by Vincent Michaels

Lf
LORIFOLK PRODUCTIONS
Melbourne, Australia
www.lorifolk.com

Published in Australia by Michael Collins
LORIFOLK PRODUCTIONS
ISBN: 978-1-7638724-1-7

For permissions or inquiries, contact: hello@lorifolk.com

National Library of Australia Cataloguing-in-Publication Data A CIP record for this book is available from the National Library of Australia.

Cover art: Foreground: Jane Francis Collins. Australian, 1955-2003 Untitled Portrait 1998 Lithograph 'Your artistry and spirit continue to inspire us.'

Background: Aurora Australis, 12 May 2024, Taroona, Tasmania. Image courtesy of Fiona Lakin.

LORIFOLK PRODUCTIONS
Melbourne, Australia
www.lorifolk.com

CONTENTS

PART THREE

BLOSSOM AND BUZZ AND THE STAIRWAY AWAY

AUTHOR'S NOTE

Lorikeet consider it polite to capitalise the names of all Folk.
Lorikeet or Lizard, Hippopotamus or Human.
    —Michael Collins

A NOTE FROM PROFESSOR FINLAY

I first met Blossom quite unexpectedly at the docks of Hobart Town, Tasmania, just as I was about to steam to Antarctica as part of a scientific expedition. Lorikeets and their cousins, the Lorifolk, have been on this earth long before my kind and are excellent talkers with those they trust. We have engaged a writer from Melbourne to assist us in telling the story of our adventures as best our recollections allow.

—Professor Conall Finlay

PROLOGUE

B efore you read about my adventure, you need to know I'm a Bird, a Rainbow Lorikeet and Human Folk generally don't treat our kind very well. And they try to tell our story, and some of what they say is true, but a lot isn't.

Then, one cold summer, it all changed.

—Blossom

PART ONE
BLOSSOM AND BUZZ AND THE TINKER OF TIME

CHAPTER I

TAROONA

The River Derwent spills out as wide as a sea as it passes Taroona, my riverside home. On the far eastern side, gently rolling green hills stretch down to the water's edge, hills that a Shore-Bird or a Wader can quickly skip across. Buzz and I are Rainbow Lorikeets, coastal Birds. We live above the cliffs on the western side of the river, high up in our nest in a hollow of a eucalyptus tree, far away from the Snakes and Cats below. At night, we hear the Derwent flap and stammer at the shore and then sigh as its waves slip back into the current.

Most mornings, I watch the Human Folk pass by in their boats, sailing up and down the river. The Dolphins and Penguins bob up and watch them as well. When Bird Folk go anywhere, it's a search for food, but Human Folk, they don't scratch and peck, dart, or dive; they talk or walk the decks, or stare at lost clouds drifting towards the horizon.

Today, the Derwent is running quicker than usual; the water is flowing in every direction all at once, just like Sparrows, scattered by a southerly wind.

"Buzz, wake up, let's go upriver again."

No answer.

"Buster, are you listening to me? I have a voice, you know!"

"You have a noise, Blossom, and don't call me Buster."

"Why not? It's your name."

No answer.

"Please, let's go upriver again, Buzz. The Human Folk in Hobart Town are so fascinating to watch, always busy and—"

He brushed aside the wattle between us.

"I'm hungry."

"You're always hungry! The town with its lights and wheels and markets and steamships and—"

"Crispy white apples at the docks."

He leapt from our branch and flew high above the Derwent.

"Come on, Blossom, I'll race you upriver."

"That's not fair. You're already on a thermal." Catching a gust of wind passing by, I glided into his airstream, and at his tail feather, I sang, "I have a voice!"

"You have a noise, Blossom."

"I'm a Rainbow Lorikeet."

"A Parrot is what you are."

"Well, I'm flying high—"

"Typical behaviour for a Bird, I think you'll find."

"High above the river," I continued, now alongside him.

"A freezing Derwent River," he replied.

Slipping under a thermal, I glided north towards Hobart Town.

"To the tall trees in the forest of ships!"

We rounded Battery Point.

Buzz flipped a wing and looped back beneath me.

"Now I'm really hungry—look," he said, dipping his wing.

"On the dock, beside the steamer, crates of delicious, crispy apples."

We dove towards the Salamanca docks at the port of Hobart and perched high on the mast of the iron steam-sailing ship, the Aurora, and watched the parade of Human Folk below, some in grey suits wearing hats, others in white dresses and bonnets. Someone called,

"Quality spectacles, German made, three and six."

A little Human Folk waved a hat and cried,

"Electric streetlights lit tonight, perfectly safe."

"Brave polar explorers, sail today," yelled another.

A steam train shrieked, the bells of the tower rang, and the Human Folk chit-chit-chatted. Above the hullabaloo, I shouted,

"Buzz, didn't I say the Human Folk are always busy and industrious?"

No answer.

"Buzz, where are you?"

I looked down to see Buzz flittering about the Human Folk who were pulling on ropes to lift an odd machine onto the Aurora's deck. A Human Folk wearing spectacles, and a blue cap shouted, "All hands! That ice sledge is precious cargo, port side, port side."

With a flip and a flap, another Human Folk, wearing a long grey dress and a black bonnet and carrying a leather case, arrived. She looked as gentle and sweet as a Dove.

A market seller bowed to her and said, "Fragrant Parisian soap for Madam Elena?"

She smiled but waved him away.

A dappled Horse pulling a cart pulled up at the gangplank. The driver shouted, "Delicious snow apples, one and six a box."

Buzz flapped.

7

A Human Folk with red hair wearing a heavy grey coat held a shiny pocket watch to the morning sun. He slapped the Human Folk with the cap and spectacles on the shoulder. "Are we on time to make this tide, Captain Lyle?"

The Captain adjusted his spectacles, squinted at the clear blue sky, and said, "Unless the moon has other plans, Professor Finlay, we'll sail on this tide."

The Professor smiled, slapped the Captain on the shoulder once again and said, "I can't control the moon on my expedition, Lyle, but time I can tinker with just a little." He struck the ship's bell three times and stood at the top of the gangplank. The crowd gathered below on the dock, all big-eyed and excited, and he called out,

"Fellow explorers, scientists, dear friends."

The crowd was silent.

"As we embark on our voyage of exploration, we turn back the page to visit a pre-industrial place of ice and snow. Through scientific inquiry, we tinker with time and read to this elderly planet a chapter, not yet written, of knowledge to better serve all creatures who share this world, now and for those that will come after us."

He held his pocket watch to the rising sun and said, "Today, we tinker with that very Human construct, that concept that is so hard to explain." He showed the watch face to the most excited gathered on the gangplank nearby and said,

"The hands on this clock are not obliged to follow the numbers as prescribed!"

The crowd squealed in delight as its hands spun like a whirlwind, and he said,

"Time starts now, and one day, the Spirits willing, we meet here again."

They all clapped and cheered, and I had an odd feeling I'd heard what he'd said before, and I smiled a Lorikeet smile.

Then, the thing they called the ice sledge landed with a thud on the deck below, and the Professor said, "Careful now, that is the only powered ice sledge in the Southern Hemisphere."

The crowd cooed and chit-chit-chatted.

"Buzz, what is an ice sledge for? And where are they going, wearing such heavy clothes?"

"To a cold, white place, without pollen or nectar to eat, just snow and—"

He flipped and flapped.

"Look, crispy white apples. I am hungry—"

Buzz swooped down and landed on an open crate of apples, pecking at one.

"What are you doing, you cheeky Bird? Be careful, or you will get—"

In a flitter, the Captain threw a fishing net over the crate of apples, trapping Buzz.

"Got you, you cheeky Bird," the Captain shouted.

"Help me, Blossom, please," Buzz called in Lorikeet song.

"Don't flap, so let me think how I can help."

The woman with the beautiful smile approached the gangplank. She looked at Buzz, all in a flip and a flap under the net and said to the Captain,

"Lyle, please no. It's such a colourful Bird, singing such a sweet song."

Smiling, the Professor guided her up the gangplank. In his arm, he carried a large box with "télégraphes" written on the side. Laughing, he said,

"Such a greedy Bird, Elena, those apples are for the crew; there are many mouths to feed on this expedition, and it's a long way to—"

The steamship bell rang. Captain Lyle called,

"All aboard who sail to Antarctica."

Elena looked at the Professor and said,

"The land of wind and ice."

"To Antarctica," said he.

"I won't have time to listen to the call of a Bird; I will be much too busy studying rocks and sending messages with this radio transmitter."

"Antarctica, so white, so cold, with wind and ice, and—"

Buzz cried a Lorikeet song.

Elena looked at Buzz again and to the Professor said,

"Conall, let's take the little Bird for luck. I can sing to its divine song. It will inspire me to finish my operetta. Our Rainbow Lorikeet in the land of white and a rainbow sky."

He smiled and, looking up to the wheelhouse, said,

"Captain Lyle, please add one Rainbow Lorikeet to the ship's manifest."

The ship's bell rang again. The Captain passed a cage to Elena, who placed a flapping Buzz inside. I gulped.

"Oh, Buzz, the land of wind and ice, what have you done!"

The ship's bell rang once again, and a crew Folk called,

"Starboard clear."

Captain Lyle, squinting, scanned the horizon.

"Steam up, clear the port side!"

The ship's bell rang again, and the crew Folk called, "Port side clear."

"We are away, Professor Finlay."

"Noted in the ship's log, Captain Dalzell, bearing due south at precisely thirteen hundred hours, on this second day of December, Nineteen hundred and eleven."

He beamed at Elena.

"Are you ready for this journey, my love?"

With a lovely smile, she stared at Buzz and said,

"No, but here I am anyway!"

Buzz flipped and flapped.

"Blossom, I don't want to sail to the cold and ice."

"Don't flap so, what use is that to a body?" I looked back towards Hobart Town.

"The town Pigeons, in that laneway—the Pigeons will help us."

"The Pigeons?" said Buzz,

"I'm doomed!"

CHAPTER 2

MR GRAY

In a flip and a flap, I landed in the middle of a flock of town Pigeons near a grimy market lane beside the Athenaeum Club. They scattered.

"Don't scatter, guys."

"We're Pigeons Blossom," chirped one of the look-alikes. "We gadder and scadder, that's what we do."

"Not today, Buzz is trapped, I need all your help." They instantly flocked around me, wide-eyed and jittery. "Don't gadder, I mean—gather guys."

At that moment, a mean Cat pounced on the flock. We all scattered.

"Well done, Snuffles," said a smartly dressed Human Folk carrying a Huon cane with a silver head on it. Snuffles jumped into his arms and watched me; there was a pocket watch hanging from his neck.

"Feathered freaks, blocking our path."

From the laneway appeared a hooded Human Folk, a Whale hunter. The ship's bell rang.

Snuffles' Human looped the cane over his wrist and, with a

small brass telescope, spied the Aurora as it steamed from the dock. He slapped the telescope into the hunter's chest.

"I want a report every month on where that steamer has been and where it is going."

The hunter sniffed and looked through the telescope—at Elena.

"Lovely—"

"Not her—" said the smartly dressed man, pushing the telescope in the direction of the Professor.

"Him! I want to know exactly what our scientist friend is up to. Do you understand anything I am saying to you?"

"I understand that you, Gray, are a pain in the—"

Snuffles growled, and his Human shoved the telescope into the Whale hunter's face.

"It's Mister Gray, actually, and if I have to sail to that frozen place because you're not doing the job I paid you to do—"

The ship's bell rang again as it steamed out of the dock.

"I heard you, Mister Gray. I report every month and keep an eye on the scientist."

Mr Gray looked at the pocket watch around Snuffles' neck.

"It's time for my morning tea."

He snatched the telescope from the hunter.

"Go away!"

The Pigeons scattered, and so did I.

CHAPTER 3
I HAVE A CHOICE

In a flip and a flap, I was back on the Aurora's mast as it steamed around Battery Point. Buzz, with his little beak between the bars of the cage, looked up at me and, with a sad look on his face, said,

"Let me guess, the Pigeons scadded?"

"Yes, the pigeons, they—but don't give up, I'll think of something."

Elena, now on the deck, picked up the cage and placed it on her lap. She stared out at lost clouds drifting towards the horizon and sang.

'Bearing south, thirteen hundred hours,
across a vast southern sea.
Am I ready, ready for this journey?
And is this journey ready for me?'

It was beautiful.

Her delicate fingers reached through the bars of the cage, and she gently stroked Buzz's beak.

'And far away, across that sea,
I see the ice, and the ice scares me.
But I have a voice, and this voice tells me,
This bird is the luck I need to sail that sea.'

Buzz looked up at me and, in Lorikeet, called,
"I'm a lucky Bird?"
She continued her song.

'It's all ice and wind and wind and ice.
And cold, I'm told and twilight night.'

Buzz flapped and called to me in Lorikeet,
"The cliffs!"
I turned to the western side of the river just as we were passing our nest in the hollow of our tree, high up on the cliffs of Taroona.
I looked down at Buzz. He looked up at me and said,
"Go! Go home before it's too late."
I looked back at our nest. I could hear the Derwent sigh as its waves slipped back into the current.
Elena continued her song.

'And far away, across that sea,
I see the ice, and the ice scares me.
And I have a voice, and this voice tells me.
This Bird is the luck that I need.'

I looked at Buzz. I looked at my home.
I swooped and perched on top of the cage and sang in Lorikeet,

'And I have a choice, and my friend and I,

will go to the land of the rainbow sky!'

"Blossom, no, that's silly," said Buzz.
Elena, slightly startled, continued her song,

> *'And I have a voice, and this voice tells me.*
> *Two Birds are luckier than one would be.*
> *Oh, we'll go to the land of the rainbow sky.'*

And together, we sang,

> *'To the rainbow sky!'*

CHAPTER 4

THE STORM

Lightning exploded above the clouds, and thunder echoed across an angry sea of blue and white. The Aurora pitched and rolled in a wild, bitterly cold wind. Captain Lyle, at the bridge, steered the ship over the mighty waves as Professor Conall, by his side, turned the rings on the machine he called a transmitter. Elena hung her head over the side, making strange noises. Buzz, still trapped inside the cage, had his head in his wings, feeling glum.

"Who would have guessed I'd feel so awful?" he called. His Lorikeet tongue hung from his beak.

Elena turned to him and said,

"Who would have thought the daughter of a navigator would get sea—? Oh, I'm going to be—"

More strange noises.

In the darkness, Professor Conall made frantic tapping sounds on his machine. Three short bursts, three long bursts, then three short again—

'dit dit dit - dat dat dat - dit dit dit,

dit dit dit - dat dat dat - dit dit dit'

The Aurora pitched and rolled as if bouncing on a sturdy branch in a wild gale. I wrapped my wings around me and spun across the wet deck.

It was bliss!

Lightning lit the sky, and the thunder clapped to my flip-pity dance until the moon appeared from under the clouds, and the sea was calm again.

CHAPTER 5
THE SHIP'S LOOKOUT

It was sunrise; the sea was so still that it joined the sky today. Buzz, feeling much better, sang Lorikeet songs from his little cage. Elena hummed along in harmony. During the night, he complained of being hungry, so I broke a twig from a branch the crew had used to sweep the deck. Buzz said it was salty, but he chewed it anyway. Later, the wind whispered to me that it was cold and would drift away from our voyage to the north. I moved from my perch on the mast to be near the warm steam blowing from the ship's funnel.

I spied on Captain Lyle at the bridge, drumming his fingers against the helm, occasionally adjusting his spectacles and rubbing his eyes.

"Ten days of storms, Conall, and only the sweet songs of those Birds to keep us merry! No sign of land yet."

He called us, 'those Birds,' again. I called out, "We do have names, you know!"

No answer.

"I'm Blossom, and that's Buzz. Let him out! We are Rainbow Lorikeets, and we have voices!"

No answer.

Human Folk who grow apples and pears back home in Taroona call us pests because we eat the fruit on the ground—though Buzz does peck at the stems, sometimes, to help them fall.

Professor Conall held a small sparkling rock and tapped at it with a tiny silver hammer.

"The life of a geologist, Lyle, is a life of tapping endless rocks."

"The life of a mariner, Conall, is a life of watching an endless horizon."

Elena took the hammer and, striking the ship's bell, sang out, "And the life of a singer is a life of endless practice."

She struck the bell once more, "But is a singer all I will ever remain?"

Captain Lyle replied, "I am a mariner; will I always sail the sea?

He struck the bell.

"Perhaps a sailor's life is not the life for me?"

Professor Conall twirled the hammer in his hand and said, "I am a geologist; I break rocks to reveal stories of nature, wind and sea, but as of this day, we're a team of explorers."

"Well, I'm just a Parrot and happy to be," said Buzz.

Professor Conall laughed. "Oh my! He's a talker! Should we let this noisy Parrot out of the cage, Captain Lyle?" He poked a piece of apple into his cage. "Is it pardoned for stealing apples? I don't think either Bird could fly far before their wings would freeze."

I flew across to the cage and bowed to him and, in my clearest Parrot voice, said,

"I am a Rainbow Lorikeet, kind sir. If you were to set my friend free, to repay your kindness and compassion, we would place our vast skill and experience as ship's lookouts at your expedition's disposal."

"What say you, Captain Lyle, two excellent lookouts to join the crew?"

"I always wanted a friendly Bird."

"We can also sing on the hour as your ship's clock," I said.

"Excellent! A ship's clock and two pairs of extra eyes. Our Crow's nest has now become our Lorikeets' nest!

Elena opened the cage.

"Out you come, my little rainbow."

Buzz, flipped, spun, and gadded and scadded and sang,

"I'm free at last! Blossom, I'm free, I'm hungry—"

He perched beside Elena, nibbling the apple.

"This one's cheeky," said Captain Lyle. "I think I will call them..."

"My mother named me Buster, but you can call me—"

"Buzz!"

The Professor looked at me.

"And what shall we call you?"

"My name is Blossom, Sir."

"Welcome to our Antarctic expedition, Blossom. It is my pleasure to meet you. Call me Conall. Something tells me you may have talents other than your vast skill and experience as a lookout."

"Thank you, Sir, I mean—"

He smiled.

"Conall."

"Yes, er—Conall. May I ask, as we sailed from the docks, you said you could tinker with time? What did you mean?"

Bravo, what a great question, Conall," said Captain Lyle.

"In my world, a tinker goes from town-to-town fixing worn-out cups, broken pots, and bent spoons."

"Then a time tinker would mend time?"

"In a way, yes." He turned to the Captain.

"Lyle, toss me that cup if you would." He threw the cup to Conall.

"Solid Tasmanian tin, that is."

"Look at this tin cup, what do you see?"

"It is an old cup."

He gave the cup to me and said, "Examine it closely."

I held the tin cup in my wings; it had a patch over a hole.

"It has a patch over a hole, just here."

"Anything else?" he said.

I turned it over.

"Oh, it has two tiny letters on it. It reads, MC."

"The maker's mark." He said, pleased. He continued,

"Now, Blossom, you could leave this cup on the deck, and over time, the salt in the sea air would oxidise it."

"Tarnish it," said Elena with a smile.

"Ah, yes." He replied to Elena knowingly. "Or you can care for it, as its maker hoped long ago, by mending its holes—"

He held it over the side and threw it into the air.

"No," I cried, swooping out and catching it.

I gave it to Captain Lyle, who filled it with water and passed it back to me. Conall continued,

"—for someone to drink from. Today, or one hundred years from today."

I drank from it.

"Now, imagine the tinker was asked to mend a ball. A ball so big it stretched across the sea and blocked the sun. And because it is so vast, it takes an exceedingly long time for the tinker to examine all its holes and think of ways to mend it. Now, for a time tinker, that ball is our Earth. We observe the world around us, examine rocks, journey to faraway places, and occasionally meet colourful Birds."

"We have been on this earth much longer than your kind," I said.

"And we can learn from you. We love knowledge; it is like a time machine, unlocking the present, the future and the past."

"But mend time?"

"When you stopped the cup from falling into the waves, you created a ripple that changed its future and its past."

Captain Lyle stepped down from the bridge and said, "Like our boat, as it steams forward, it makes waves behind it that will eventually reach a distant shore."

"Our earth is old," said Conall.

"But its story has not yet been told, and you and I can change the story. When we tinker with time, we find and patch the holes and rewrite what once was on the page before."

How curious, I thought. "Human Folk are so fascinating."

Captain Lyle slapped Conall on the back and, looking at me, said,

"Perhaps, one day, Conall can show you his inventions. What do you think?"

"I would love that!"

"It is a promise, then," said Conall.

Captain Lyle put the cage under a tarpaulin.

"Now, my Lorikeet friends, up you fly into the ship's lookout to earn your keep."

"You mean the Lorikeets' lookout," said a grinning Buzz.

Captain Lyle laughed.

"I stand corrected. The Lorikeets' lookout—cheeky Bird."

And in a flip and a flap, we flew to our new home, high above the Aurora, where the sea and the sky were one.

CHAPTER 6

AN ISLAND

It was twilight. Elena practised her singing; Buzz flapped around her. I watched them. Elena sang out a musical note to Buzz.

"That's an A," said Buzz, with a silly smile on his beak.

"Oui," said Elena, in a different Human Folk tongue.

She sang a higher note to Buzz.

"That's a B," said Buzz.

"Si, I mean, yes!" She sang a third note to him. I listened closely; it was lower. Buzz held his wingtip to his beak, pretending he was thinking ever so hard.

"That's definitely a D," said Buzz.

"Correct," she said, stroking his head.

"It's nice to agree," he said.

"Oui, si and yes, Buzzy."

My feathers bristled.

"Aargh!"

Buzz frowned at me.

"Blossom, that's an A flat; we're not doing those."

Elena sang out another note to Buzz.

"That's definitely an F," said Buzz, impressed with himself.

"Correct!" said Elena, in her tongue this time.

I coughed.

Buzz frowned at me—again.

"Did you say something, Blossom?"

"Moi? Non."

They continued their silly game until Conall, looking through binoculars on the bridge, called.

"Lyle, Elena, it's Macquarie Island." He pointed towards the fog.

"We are halfway to Antarctica."

I looked out beyond the mist, and a long green hill appeared, flat on top with yellow tinges and a rocky-black shore. Buzz nudged me in the side.

"Look, Blossom, along the shore, waddling Birds, their feathers black and white and—"

I looked at the shoreline.

"Orange! Buzz, they're Royal Penguins, our Bird cousins. Let's go say hello!"

I jumped into a thermal.

Buzz, in flight, turned back towards our new friends and, with a beaming smile, called, "Back soon, Conall, Captain Lyle —back soon, Elena."

CHAPTER 7
A ROYAL COUSIN

We arrived at the island shore in a flip and a flap. Thousands of Royal Penguins gathered around a tall, noble Penguin with a fine silver and orange crown of feathers on her head. We approached her, bowing awkwardly.

"Umm, hello. My name is Blossom. May I introduce you to my friend Buzz? We are Rainbow Lorikeets from far North of here."

"I am Princess Patagonicus, daughter of the Queen and King of all Royal Penguins. Rainbow Lorikeets are welcome to our land."

A Penguin Folk with a feathery orange spike on their head gave us a sweet-smelling drink from a silvery jug.

"Some honey nectar to drink?"

"Thank you," I said, accepting the drink. "It is an honour to meet you, Princess."

"You rule over lots of Penguins, Princess," said Buzz. "More Penguins than we ever see at home in Taroona."

"My mother and father swore to preserve our colony from the feared Lamplighters."

"Lamplighters?" said Buzz between gulps of honey nectar.

"Misguided Human folk who hunt and kill us to make oil to light their lanterns."

The Princess directed us to a rocky platform with shimmering stone seats overlooking the curved bay.

"As I speak, the King and Queen are searching the East and West coasts for many of our kind who are missing."

"That is hideous, Princess," I said. "How can Human Folk be so cruel?"

She turned towards the coast and said.

"We pray to the souls of our ancestors for guidance and protection. Now, please rest. You are both a long way from home, Rainbow Lorikeets."

Buzz sat opposite her. He pointed his wing at our steamer, anchored out in the bay.

"We're explorers, sailing with Captain Lyle on his steamship, the Aurora, to Antarctica, the land of wind and ice."

"To see the Rainbow Lights," I added.

"The Rainbow Lights?" The Princess raised her flipper to the sky.

"It is said the Rainbow Lights are the souls of our Penguin kind, dancing in the night sky with the souls of the great Blue Whales and Grey Seals. All stolen from us by the Lamplighters."

She paused, and the Penguins surrounding her bowed their heads in silence.

"You have a long journey to the land of wind and ice, my young explorers. It is much colder there. What do you eat? Food from the land and the sea?"

"Pollen and nectar from the flowering treetops beside the Derwent River," I said.

"Princess, have you seen the Rainbow Lights before?" I asked.

"I have not been so blessed."

She turned to Buzz.

"And you, my friend, do you also eat pollen and nectar?"

"I like crispy white apples from the Hobart dockside."

"I'm afraid there will be very few crispy white apples in Antarctica. But perhaps if you travel to Mount Erebus, you will find the Pearl Wheel."

"Pearl, what?" said a rather puzzled Buzz.

"Pearl Wheel. It is the only flower in Antarctica; its pollen is said to be magical."

Buzz eyed the large silver jug of the delightful nectar.

"More honey nectar?"

"Thank you, Your Highness."

"Enough of the—Your Highness, please. I'm a Bird cousin to you both; you may call me Cousin Pat."

"Cousin—Pat?" Buzz repeated.

"Yes, of course. We aren't that different from you." The Princess—Cousin Pat stretched out her long, sleek, black, powerful wings.

"We also have wings."

"We've got wings," said Buzz with a flap.

"We've got beaks," said Cousin Pat.

"We've got beaks," I added.

The Princess pointed to her feathers.

"We've got black and white and orange feathers."

"We've got orange too—"

"Well, mostly green," said Buzz, unnecessarily. The Princess laughed.

"See, we aren't that different from you. We're just the Penguin side of your family."

"Well, it's a pleasure to be the Parrot side of your family," said Buzz.

A distant bell rang. Princess Pat stood.

"The ship's bell! Quickly, you are sailing; you must fly back and join Captain Lyle."

"And Professor Conall, he's a geologist," I said.

"And Professor Conall, the geologist," said Princess Pat.

Buzz stood.

"And Elena, the singer. She is composing an operetta, you know!"

"And—Elena, the singer and composer. Hurry now if you wish to join them on your adventure. Remember, we are all family."

A large jar was passed to me by one of the Penguin Folk.

"And take this: it should keep you from getting hungry on your adventure. Be safe on your journey of discovery, my friends!"

"Goodbye, Cousin Pat, and thank you. May your Folk be secure and your future always bright. If we can ever be of service to you, please don't hesitate to call out."

In a flip and a flap, we flew back towards the Aurora. As we approached the ship, I noticed a figure on a distant ice flow.

"That's curious," I thought out loud.

As Buzz landed on the deck, I quickly dipped a wing and turned towards the ice flow.

CHAPTER 8
THE LAMPLIGHTER

I landed awkwardly in a pool of water on an ice flow behind a cloaked man holding a heavy stick with a lantern at the top.

"Is anybody out there?" he said gruffly as he raised the lantern.

I held my breath. A Lamplighter!

My foot stuck to the ice.

Then the well-dressed man with the mean Cat that the Pigeons and I saw in Hobart approached. He wore a thick coat and dark goggles.

"Oh, it's you, Gr—Mr Gray," spat the Lamplighter.

Mr Gray pointed his cane with the silver head at the Lamplighter.

"Have you finished your count of my stock yet? I don't fancy giving up my blanket to you on another bitter night in this freezing hell!"

The Lamplighter raised his lantern in anger.

"I would be very careful with what you say next, Lamplighter," said Gray, striking the ice with his cane that opened up a crack.

"Not yet—Mr Gray," said the Lamplighter through clenched teeth.

Their eyes followed the expanding crack as it advanced towards me. I tugged extra hard at my foot, kicking it free, and in a flitter, I launched into the sky and was gone.

CHAPTER 9
EXPLORER BUZZ

We sailed for many days and nights towards Antarctica. Our Lorikeet lookout was too cold and icy to sleep in, so Conall built us a nest. He used a sack with MERINO WOOL stamped on it.

I flew around the Aurora's bow to stretch my wings. Captain Lyle reached for his telescope.

"This damn fog, I can't see a thing."

Buzz swooped down, sat on the helm and saluted Captain Lyle.

"I'm a great spotter, Captain. Do you need me to search the waters for you?"

He took off his cap and scratched his head.

"We do have a problem. This icy Antarctic coast is much too shallow to go ashore." He turned to Buzz.

"I need you to fly high over the masts, above the fog, to see what I can't see down here."

"Yes, sir," said Buzz. His feathers were quivering. "Fly high above the fog."

"Now, Buzz, this calm weather won't last. Before long, the icy winds will be upon us."

"Yes, Captain."

"And Buzz, here in the Southern Ocean, we are at the very edge of the known world. Be careful. Keep calling so we know you are safe."

"Aye-aye, Captain, I'll find our safe harbour."

I thought about the Lamplighter on the ice flow near Macquarie Island and flapped at the Captain,

"I should go, Captain Lyle, not Buzz. We don't know what or who is out there. I can fly just as swiftly, and my eyes are very sharp. I'll find us a safe harbour."

"Well, I mean, you're an excellent lookout as well, of course."

Buzz nudged me hard.

"I think the Captain gave me an order, Blossom."

In a flip and a flap, he had climbed high above us, his calls fading into the distance.

"Be safe, cheeky Bird," said the Captain, raising his telescope to the sky.

Buzz faded into the fog. "Be careful," I called, wishing I hadn't let him go alone.

Captain Lyle turned to me with a wilting smile. "He'll be okay, won't he?"

"Buzz will stay close, I'm sure. Lorikeets believe if we fly too far, we will cross the edge of time and enter the unknown."

Captain Lyle lowered his telescope.

"As a boy, I often dreamt I'd fall from the world if I sailed too close to the horizon. As I fell, my billowing sails would become entangled on a nearby star, and I'd spin like a bauble on a Christmas tree, waiting to be rescued by an angel."

The wind began to stir. We both looked for Buzz.

I left Captain Lyle on the bridge and found Conall in the

galley, seated at a table with assorted contraptions and gadgets. Elena arrived with a mug of steaming cocoa.

"Here you are, Professor Finlay."

She examined the contraptions.

"I can understand that a transmitter and the electric searchlight are vital for our sea voyage, but this microscope and those brass scales, what do you hope to find in Antarctica?"

"Dolerite, my love."

"Oh, how silly of me. Dolerite, that rare plant—"

"Mineral."

"Mineral found in the—ice."

"Rocky cliffs of Antarctica."

"Oh, Rocky cliffs. Exactly."

I tapped at the scales; they swung back and forth in rhythm with the rolling ship. Elena turned to me.

"Blossom, you're back. Is Buzz with you?"

"He's trying to find us a safe harbour."

"Conall, didn't you say storms are nearby?"

Conall adjusted the searchlight.

"He's a resourceful little Bird, that one. Let's go up on deck. This searchlight is the latest thing in electricity and needs a test."

Why did I let him go on his own?

CHAPTER 10
FEATHERS DON'T FREEZE

A s I stood on the deck, the wind whispered to me—
'Buzz is soaring over cliffs of ice, searching for
safe shelter. He is calling,—'

'Feathers don't freeze in the icy breeze.
I'm warm and dry, high in the sky.
This fog is only a gentle light mist.
A harbour, a beach, not to be missed.

Look left, look right, look down below.
Captain Lyle told me so.

Be strong, try hard and don't give up just yet.
Be calm, stay focused. There's no time to fret.
This fog is only a gentle light mist—
a harbour, a beach, not to be missed.

I'm feeling tired, I'm feeling weak.
The ice is freezing my Lorikeet beak.

My wings are heavy; my eyes are sore.
A harbour, a beach, I think no more—'

"Oh, no!"

In a flip and a flap, I climbed high into the thick fog and shadowed the trail of Buzz's faded calls. The wind swirled about me, and ice stuck to my wingtips.

"Hold on, Buzz," I called. "Just a little longer, a few more flaps, I'll find you."

I searched the giant sea map below me. He was nowhere to be seen.

"Be strong, Buzz, don't give up."

I soared over a thermal and rolled under a thick cloud. A searchlight flashed through the mist. Suddenly, a flitter of orange, green, red, and blue tumbled past me, towards the water.

"Buzz!"

I dove to him, stretching my wings under his limp body.

"Blossom," he withered, "Is it you? Look left, look right, look—" he faded.

"Don't give up, Buzz, we can do it! A harbour, a beach, not to be missed."

Dazed but flying, he shook his feathers out, rolled through the fog and chirped,

"Blossom, down there, below the mist. Is it a harbour we nearly missed?"

I looked; it was Antarctica!

"There is a harbour—way below, with a rocky beach and an icy shore."

"Are you sure it's a shore?" He croaked.

"I'm sure, I'm sure. It's not like I've never seen a shore before."

We flew together towards the rocky beach.

"Buzz, you did it. You've found a safe port for the Aurora."

He flapped his wing around me as we landed on the Antarctic shore.

"We found it together; you saved my life, Blossom." He sank to the ground, exhausted.

I flapped my wing right back at him.

"We worked together as a good crew should."

CHAPTER II
OUR ANTARCTIC CAMP

Buzz slept until sunrise, with just a few drowsy mumbles of, 'Look left, look right,' or 'Captain Lyle told me so.' Our Antarctic camp was a nest of huts, little boats, crates, sledges, and ropes on a small rocky shoreline—sea ice in one direction, still blue water beyond that and snow-covered hills everywhere else. Captain Lyle came out of his hut. He wore a bushy hat and thick clothes.

"I see my heroic crew members are up and about camp already. How commendable." When he talked, little clouds of fog came from his mouth.

"There's no time to rest on this adventure," I said as icy air whirled about my Lorikeet beak.

He warmed his hands by the fire.

"After your superb effort getting us here, you deserve a hearty meal."

Buzz, wrapping his feathers extra tight around himself, hopped towards Captain Lyle.

"Blossom and I are about to go and search for our breakfast. Pearl Wheel flower. It's the only flowering plant in

Antarctica. It's growing somewhere near that mountain behind us."

"Mount Erebus?" said Captain Lyle.

"Yes," I said, "Princess Pat told us Pearl Wheel pollen is magical."

"Magical, you say? Well, you must find this Pearl Wheel flower, our first floral specimen to bring home to impress the botanists back at Hobart. Buzz, come, I'll give you a canvas bag to carry it."

"Morning, all," called Conall as he picked through rocks along the shore. He reminded me of our Magpie friends back home in Taroona. Now and then, he'd pick a rock up, inspect it, and place it in a canvas bag.

Elena, wrapped in a heavy coat and waving a glass ring, skipped across to me and said,

"He forgot his magnifying glass. Let's visit a scientist at work."

I followed her towards the shore. Conall approached us, holding out a shiny rock in the palm of his gloved hand.

"Look at this rock, my love. Do you notice something unusual about it?"

Elena frowned.

"It's just another one of the thousands of rocks scattered along this shore."

"But it's not. This rock, what we geologists call a metamorphic rock, is actually from the shoreline near Hobart. I packed it with me, yet it's identical to the rocks at our feet. Curious, don't you think?"

"But how can it be the same?"

"Once upon a time, Antarctica was joined to Australia—the supercontinent called Gondwana. But, millions of years ago, time-tinkered, and it broke apart, perhaps splitting right here on this very shore.

He extended his arm and, with his finger, drew an imaginary line along the shore beside us. He then picked up a rock and continued.

"Australia began slowly drifting north, resting where it is today. This beach and these rocks have their twins in Hobart." He pointed towards a ridge of cliffs in the distance. "There are dolerite rock columns over there, just like those at the Organ Pipes at Mount Wellington in Hobart."

"At Kunanyi?" said Elena.

"The very same," he replied, looking at the twin rocks in each hand. "What secrets do you both have to tell, I wonder?" He moved them closer to each other. "Of the past, the present, and the future?" The rocks quivered, and a faint hum floated through the air. "How curious—"

"What's that sound?" said Elena, turning to the source. "Conall, why are the rocks vibrating?"

Conall then spoke in an odd, dream-like voice. "The nickel-iron rechargeable battery, having an electrolyte of potassium hydroxide—"

"I beg your pardon," said Elena.

Conall shook his head, alert as an Eagle. "It just came into my head at this moment, the properties that make up a rechargeable battery to power the electric searchlight. It's an idea I was working on this morning. I couldn't determine what electrolyte to use; it is potassium hydroxide! I wonder, do these rocks—"

Elena pointed to the vibrating rocks. "Ok, Conall, potassium—whatever you said—but why are these rocks vibrating?" Her pointing finger began to shake. She sang a note as high as the clouds and clear as a bell, echoing along the icy shore. "And why can I now sing the high G I couldn't reach during my morning practice?"

"How very curious," said Conall. "Blossom, Buzz, come and have a closer look, friends."

"What odd rocks," said Buzz.

"Yes, we think so as well," said Conall.

"I feel all tingly inside," said Buzz, pointing to the mountain behind us. In an odd sing-song, he called, "Three Pearl Wheel flowers are growing in a small cave at the base of that Mount Erebus mountain, that way!

"How did I know that?" said Buzz, suddenly himself again.

I turned to Conall. "Conall, Elena, how does he know that? We haven't left our camp yet."

"No, it couldn't, but then, how curious," said Conall.

Elena looked at Conall and said, "You're not speaking what you're thinking—again."

He looked in deep thought, then said.

"There is a scientific law that objects with opposite electric charge attract, and objects with the same electric charge, like these rocks in my hand, repel each other."

"Sounds like some friendships I've known," said Elena.

He laughed awkwardly. "But here on this icy shore, where one continent fractured long ago, the law of attraction and repulsion is affecting us. Our future knowledge is rapidly being drawn towards our present."

"So, we are learning?" said Elena.

"At a vastly accelerated rate," replied Conall.

The rocks shook again. I suddenly felt all dreamy inside. My feathers flittered and flapped. "Oh no!" I called. "Princess Patagonicus is in trouble!"

"Cousin Pat?" said Buzz.

"She needs us urgently; the Lamplighters are approaching her island in boats. We must hurry!"

CHAPTER 12

TO THE RESCUE

A long, hollow pipe pointed skyward from the deck of the Aurora. Conall busily connected wires to it.

"Now, Blossom, listen carefully," he said.

"I've built this cannon from the fuselage of the ice sledge. Put this helmet on and slowly climb up, and slide into it, with your head sticking out the end."

I did as I was told.

"Wait," said Buzz. "One of the crew made these goggles for me; you wear them, Blossom."

"In theory," said Conall, as he connected more wires and twisted dials, "My amplitude modulator machine should work fine."

"What exactly does, in theory, mean, Conall?" Buzz asked.

Elena replied. "It means we won't know if it will work until after we fire it."

My feathers flapped. Conall continued.

"If the radio receiver I left on Macquarie Island is still working and—"

He placed two vibrating rocks in a box.

"—these twin, metamorphic rocks create sufficient spark in the battery to push an electromagnetic radio wave from inside the cannon—"

He strapped the box to the cannon.

"—it should propel Blossom, at one hundred and twenty-five miles per second, on an electron modulating bridge, to the Palace of Princess Patagonicus, which I've calculated to be one thousand miles away—"

He looked at his pocket watch.

"—in precisely nine, point-four seconds."

"Blossom, can I have my goggles back?" called Buzz.

Captain Lyle frowned. "Not nice, Buzz."

"Sorry, Captain. Blossom, you can keep the—"

"It's okay, Buzz." I took a deep breath, "Let's do this, Professor, Cousin Pat needs our help!"

Conall held up his pocket watch and pointed his thumb at me, and counted—

"Ten, nine, eight—"

"Cover your ears all," shouted Captain Lyle, with his hands over his ears.

Elena covered her ears and called to me.

"Good luck, Blossom!"

My beak was all jittery.

"Seven, six, five—"

"They were my only pair of goggles—" added Buzz.

"Four, three, two, one—Fire!"

My heart skipped a beat as I shot out of the cannon. Sparks followed me. Everything but my destination blurred. Faster, higher, then—

—In a flip and a flap, I could see the Royal Penguins waving to me from the shore below. Cousin Pat called—

"Our loyal Lorikeet cousin has come to help us!"

Conall's plan had worked.

CHAPTER 13

FROM THERE TO HERE

A flock of Royal Penguins escorted me up the steep steps of the Palace, carved deep into the rocky cliffs of Macquarie Island. More Penguins gathered at the square, nodding gloomily to me as I passed through the vast Palace doors. Princess Pat was seated on her magnificent black and white throne, surrounded by Penguin Folk reading maps and charts. She looked ever-so-regal, but I could tell she was uneasy.

"Blossom, you're here; come, sit with me."

I did so. Princess Pat continued.

"A party of Penguins, led by my mother, the Queen, is missing, and Father is desperately searching for her. We have received reports that the Lamplighters are off the coast, only hours away. Blossom, you must help stop them from taking more of our kind."

"Yes, of course, I will. If Conall were here, he could help—"

A loud crack rang out, and Conall and Elena casually walked through the Palace doors, goggles around their necks. Conall, with his pocket watch in hand, said,

"Eight, point four-eight seconds exactly, that's twenty-thousand feet per second, very impressive."

Elena looked over her shoulder and said,

"Where's Buzz? He was right behind me."

There was a crashing sound, and Buzz appeared, crawling up the steps.

"I lost one of my tail feathers!"

"Oh, poor Buzz, it's so brave of you all to come and help us," said Princess Pat.

A Royal Penguin passed the Princess a note on a silver plate.

"It's from my father, the King. I have feared the arrival of this letter for many days now—I can't read it. Please, Madam Elena, would you?"

"Of course, I will, Princess. It reads—

'My darling daughter, I have received word that your mother, our Queen, has been taken away on the boat of a Lamplighter. We will search every moment of every day, henceforth, for her safe return.'

The Penguins clucked and stomped their feet.

"Oh, Princess," said Elena. "Your mother, the Queen. We must do all we can to rescue her. Conall, we need to stop the Lamplighters, and quickly."

"Princess," said Conall, "Our previous expedition stored some searchlights and a boat when last here. If we work together—"

"We'll stop the Lamplighters," I said.

"Blossom, I need you to help me with the radio transmitter."

"I'm ready, Professor."

"Buzz, there's a hut a little way along the shore; the search-light and boat are in it. Elena will help you."

"Yes, sir!"

Princess Pat stood.

"Thank you, Professor, Madam Elena, and my dear Lori-keet cousins. I shall send word to my father of your assistance, and he will find a way to get a message to Mother. Our Queen and King are forever in your debt; Royal Penguins never forget the kindness shown to them in times of need. There are many things I forgot to do and say to my mother when she walked out those doors. It is not the time for her colours to be painted in the Rainbow Sky. Bring her home to me, please, set her free."

CHAPTER 14

AT SEA, OFF THE COAST OF MACQUARIE ISLAND

In the fading daylight, our rowboat made its way through the cracks and gaps of the ice as it headed offshore from the Royal Palace. The Penguins, Wales, and Seals tailed us to provide protection. Buzz helped Conall and Elena shine the searchlight in the direction of where the Lamplighters were last seen.

"Is anybody out there?" I called.

No answer.

"Over there, on that ice flow," said Elena. "Their lanterns are moving."

"Where?" said Buzz, rocking our little boat excitedly.

"Can anyone hear me? I'm Conall Finlay, geologist and time-tinker from the expedition ship Aurora. We are collecting rare Bird species."

"Rare Birds, you say, Mr Finlay," said a croaky, jagged voice in the distance.

"Yes, the Rainbow Lorikeet."

Buzz looked at Conall, confused.

"But you're not collecting Rainbow—"

"Buzz, play along," I whispered. "We have a plan."

"Where are you, Mr Finlay?"

"Three o'clock to you."

"We've not sighted any Bird of that name, but we have rare Birds."

Conall turned the searchlight onto me, projecting my shadow on an iceberg near where lanterns were moving.

"We only seek the—"

"The Lamplighters are moving nearer to us," said Elena.

"Where are you now, Mr Finlay?"

"Six o'clock."

"The Patagonicus Penguin is very rare."

The voice was much closer to us now. Elena whispered to Buzz that they were taking the bait. Conall turned the searchlight off and called,

"We are not familiar with that Penguin species. Show us."

Five boat lengths away, dimly lit by the lanterns, a group of Royal Penguins huddled on the ice. Elena reached for Conall's hand.

"Oh, my Conall, Queen Patagonicus is with them. Princess Pat looks so much like her mother."

The croaky voice continued.

"Perhaps you'd entertain trading with the Lamplighters, Mr Finlay?"

"A trade, you say?"

"What say you?"

We all held our breath, waiting for Conall's reply. We shone the searchlight on the Penguins.

"What can we trade to a Lamplighter that's fair? What do we have as equally rare?"

"What is that light that shines so bright?"

48

"This light, you mean, with its powerful beam."

"A light that bright, we have never seen."

"It is an electric light that shines one hundred times brighter than your lantern flame."

"That I can see, and I can see a trade, but can we agree?"

"What terms, say you, for a light that outshines a hundred times?"

"One hundred Penguins right now for that electric light. They're my terms; I'll bargain this cold, icy night."

"We accept your trade," said Conall. "But we can sweeten the deal. Would one hundred lights be of appeal?"

"One hundred lights! Indeed, it would, but I've no more to trade, even if I could."

Conall paused a moment and then called out—

"Perhaps Whale or Seal, you know?"

The Lamplighter replied—

"One thousand Seals and fifty Whales are located north, in the Bay of Gales."

"I can trade one hundred lights for your Penguin, Seal and Whale hunting rights."

Conall continued—

"The electric light has no need for oil, no need to hunt in the cold and toil."

The Lamplighter stepped into the searchlight and held his lantern up high.

"We accept your trade, which has great appeal, but I insist we sign and seal such a deal. We meet at Mount Erebus in ten days."

Conall stood up.

"Agreed, beneath the lights of the Rainbow Sky."

Queen Patagonicus stepped forward into the searchlight and said,

"And we call as envoys for both sides. Two, who are not Penguin, Whale, Seal or Humankind. But have rainbow hearts and open minds. The Rainbow Lorikeets will seal this deal for all of time."

CHAPTER 15
RAINBOW HEARTS AND OPEN MINDS

With a thousand squeals and clicks, Macquarie Island's Royal Penguins welcomed Queen Patagonicus back to the Palace. Conall and Elena received kind nods as they passed through the crowds, their path swept free of rocks by Penguin tails. Much to our surprise, Buzz and I were carried up the steps of the Palace on the shoulders of some younger Penguins, enchanted by our green-coloured feathers. There were long speeches by the Queen and King, and Princess Pat explained how two Rainbow Lorikeets from the north became crew on an unlikely voyage to Antarctica, and Buzz must have drunk two jugs of honey nectar! After much partying, we camped in an old hut and explored the Island with our Penguin cousins while we waited for the Aurora to return us to Antarctica for the summit in ten days.

Our return journey to Antarctica on the Aurora was not as thrilling as my cannon shot to Macquarie Island, but it was much fun with our Penguin passengers. We arrived at Antarctica on the day of the summit, and everyone helped prepare for the guests: Whales and Seals, Penguins and Lamplighters, Human Folk and Lorikeets.

There was one problem, and it was a big one.

"Buzz, I don't know how to be an envoy! What if we make a mistake at the summit today? What if they laugh at us?"

"What if I ask Elena to be the envoy?" said Buzz. "Or Captain Lyle? He's wise."

"Did someone say, Captain Lyle? I've heard much news of your adventures, my chattering friends. Why am I not surprised you rescued the Queen?"

"Captain, thank goodness," I said. "My heart's beating so fast. I'm in a flap,"

"I feel all dizzy," said Buzz. "We're worried this day won't end well at all."

Captain Lyle sat on a piece of driftwood and gathered us in.

"Slow down—what's the problem? Why are you worried today won't end well?"

"I have no voice," I said.

"We're Parrots, just all noise," said Buzz.

"You're both beautiful Rainbow Lorikeets with rainbow hearts and open minds, remember that at the summit today!"

Buzz flapped. Captain Lyle stood and asked Buzz to sit with me.

"Inside your chest, you have a space," he said, placing his hand on his chest. "It's like a room—or a balloon, where air flows in and out, in equal pace. And we have a handle to control our breathing." He raised his hands to his head. "It's like a lever."

"Let me show you; stand up, my Lorikeet friends. Now, breathe in and lift the lever to your nose—"

"But we don't have a nose," said Buzz.

"Do what I do," said Captain Lyle.

"Breathe in, lift your wings to your beak—Breathe out, let your wings fall to your feet."

I breathed in and lifted my wings to my beak. Buzz did the same. We breathed out and let our wings fall to our feet.

"I'm feeling a little better," said Buzz.

"Keep going," said Captain Lyle, raising and lowering his arms with each breath.

"Did I mention the wheel?"

"What wheel?" said I.

"A wheel that adjusts how I feel. Below my head, there's a wheel; it's called a neck."

"We have a neck," said Buzz.

"You both do—and this neck is a wheel that adjusts how we feel. It's a compass, I guess, to east and west."

"And north and south?" I asked.

"Yes!" said the Captain, raising and lowering his hands with each breath.

"East is sad, frown, I might. West is best; I'm happy and bright! And north and south? Neither worst nor best, in the middle, I suppose. There's no rule, I guess."

"So, my Lorikeet friends, Breathe in and—"

"Lift the lever to my beak," said Buzz.

"Breathe out—"

"Let it fall to my feet," said I.

"East—"

"I frown, just a bit," said Buzz.

"West—"

"It is funny," I admit.

Captain Lyle adjusted his glasses and said,

"And everything else, in between, is who we are and what we've been. Happy and sad, worried and strong, come and go and dance along. You both have a voice—remember to breathe.

You're beautiful, Rainbow Lorikeets with rainbow hearts and open minds."

I looked at Buzz; he looked at me, and together, we said—

"We have rainbow hearts and open minds."

CHAPTER 16
LORIKEET ENVOYS

Buzz and I nervously waited in our seats at the summit table. The Royal Penguins encircled us, crowded on the rocky Antarctic shore. From the icy bay, Whales and Seals watched on, together with Lamplighters in their long boats and the crew of our steamship, the Aurora. Princess Pat is seated on my right, and a Lamplighter is to our left. The Queen and King, Conall, Elena, and Captain Lyle are seated in front, along with hundreds more Lamplighters and thousands more Penguins. The sky shifted to twilight pink above Mount Erebus behind us.

I looked to the west at the crowded shore and took a big breath. Captain Lyle raised his hands and, smiling, nodded to us.

I stood, stretched out my wings and began.

"Lamplighter, how many of your folk have drowned at sea in your search for oil?

"Many have, Lorikeet."

"And how many of your folk have starved on the ice?"

"Many more."

Buzz stood and said,

"Or been crushed by the great Whale?"

"Yes, we have lost many of our folk searching for the oil."

"And why do you need the oil?" I asked.

"To light our lanterns."

"But you have the sun to light your way."

"We cannot see in the dark of night."

Buzz then asked,

"Why not sleep when the sun sleeps?"

"When the sun sleeps, we eat, read, laugh, and sing."

I passed the agreement prepared by Elena and Princess Pat to the Lamplighter and said—

"Lamplighter, have you agreed to trade your rights to hunt the Penguins, Whales, and Seals gathered here around you today, in exchange for one hundred and one electric lights?"

"A light that needs no oil, yet burns bright throughout the night," said Conall.

"Your folk will not need to starve or drown," said I.

The Lamplighter stood and, passing me the agreement, said,

"We agree and desire to be at peace with Whale, Seal and Penguin folk."

"Princess," I asked. "Do you agree to this trade?"

She stood.

"We, the Royal Penguins, agree."

I looked at the Lamplighter and said, "Lamplighter, do you understand that these hunting rights you trade will be extinguished for all time?"

"We understand."

I turned to the crowd on the shore and in the bay and said,

"What say you, the great Blue Whales, the Grey Seals and the Penguin folk?"

A chorus of flaps and calls rang out. Buzz raised his wings and said,

"The Voices of the Rainbow Sky agree."

I held the agreement above my head and called out, "Then we have resolved this matter, on this day, at this hour, under the lights of the Rainbow Sky. Witnessed by all present here."

"Hooray!" shouted Buzz.

Everyone clapped, flapped, cheered, and called. Princess Pat thanked us, and we told her we would return home to Taroona once we had helped Conall build the electric lights.

CHAPTER 17
GOODBYE RAINBOW SKY

The ship's bell rang, and Captain Lyle called from the bridge, "We sail on the incoming tide!"

Glancing at his pocket watch, Conall added, "Load the Aurora, everyone. We are Hobart-bound in one hundred and eighty minutes precisely!"

He then turned to the Princess and, with a little bow, said, "Princess, your loyal subjects have been most kind in helping us build the electric lights for the Lamplighters."

Princess Pat smiled and, returning the bow, said, "My Rainbow Lorikeet cousins are always welcome at our Palace, as are you, Professor Finlay, Madam Elena and Captain Lyle."

We all said our goodbyes, and one hundred and eighty minutes later, we steamed from Antarctica, homeward bound.

CHAPTER 18

HOME AGAIN

The Dolphins and Penguins bobbed up and watched me, with the Human Folk, sail up the River Derwent to Hobart Town. Near the stern, Buzz stared at lost clouds drifting towards the horizon.

"Conall, may I ask you a question?"

"Of course, Blossom, what is it?"

"What does it feel like to be a Human?"

"Oh, well—that is a curious but excellent question! To be Human is—well, it's—I mean, I was born a baby Human, so it's all I've ever known— you understand? What does it feel like to be a Human?"

"Some Humans aren't very kind to one another, are they?" I asked.

"That's true. May I ask why are you—"

And just then, above the cliffs, on the western side of the river, high up in the hollow of a eucalyptus tree, I saw our nest, far away from the Snakes and Cats below.

"Look, everyone, our home, the treetops of Taroona! Elena, Captain Lyle, Conall, look!"

Buzz and I jumped onto a thermal and, in a flip and a flap, were in our nest. It made me feel so happy, all amongst the twisting wood, in my soft, safe place of twigs and love, where broken things mend.

And, that first night home from our Antarctic adventure, Buzz didn't complain about being hungry, and as the wind began to stir and the Owls commenced their shift, we tucked our heads beneath our wings in a kind of sleepy drift.

And a sweet song filled the air, and we slept until the dawn.

PART TWO
BLOSSOM AND BUZZ AND THE TEMPO SPIRALE

CHAPTER 19
ONE YEAR LATER

It's been one whole year, or as Conall said at our party at the Salamanca Docks last night, 'Eight thousand, seven hundred and eighty-four hours precisely!' since we came back from our Antarctic adventure in the land of ice and snow.

Captain Lyle is still a captain in Hobart Town and lives in his boat in Sandy Bay. Buzz often helps him navigate around. Elena is a singing teacher at a friendly school and lives in Claremont. Buzz and I assist Conall with his experiments in his workshop. Last week, it was about spiral equations and geothermal, tectonic abrasions.

Cousin Pat often sends messages of hello from Macquarie Island, and the Lamplighters remain as friends, not foes.

Everything is good in our world.

Elena did say there have been rumblings from across the seas. A Human Folk War? But I have no worries; Tasmania is divine with all our friends.

Today, Buzz and I are flying downriver to Conall's workshop to help with an experiment to convert power—while we're in a metal nest!

In a flip and a flap, we landed on the roof of the workshop and tapped seven times on the lightning rod. A skylight opened, and we went in.

"Welcome back, my Lorikeet helpers," said Conall, a metal spike in one gloved hand and a tiny spinning wheel in the other.

"Let's get you two strapped in!"

Conall fastened Buzz and me side-by-side inside a glowing, nest-like metal cage and tapped dials and turned knobs on his control panel. Then, for quite a while, he threw switches and pulled levers.

"Now, you two, you must stop chatting. I can't hear myself think! Temporal Energy Accelerators are not toys."

"Move, Buzz! You're squashing me," I said.

"Blossom, Buzz, I need you both to focus, please! That metal orb must capture the energy from your body heat at exactly the right resonance to enable transfer to the battery storage."

It was very tight in the metal nest.

"Blossom, would you stop wriggling so?" said Buzz.

"Conall, do I push this lever or pull that one?" I asked.

Buzz pointed to the knob in front of me. "You turn that knob, Blossom, but only after I have pulled this lever."

"Are you sure, Buzz?"

"I'm sure. Professor Finlay, we are ready for launch."

I wasn't so sure. Conall held up his stopwatch and started to count down.

"Ten, nine, eight, seven—"

The orb spun and glowed. Buzz reached for the lever and said, "Activating nest accelerator in three, two—"

I turned the knob.

"Blossom, no, don't turn it yet—"

The windows began to rattle, and the workshop shook. I

could hear a far-off rumbling sound. Conall heard it too and said, "What's that—is it thunder?"

The shaking got much worse, and Conall was having difficulty standing.

"Conall, why are we shaking so?" I said.

"I'm not sure; it could be a temporal disturbance of some kind."

"My beak feels all tingly," said Buzz.

I could feel a change inside me, and I sensed doubt. My wings felt odd, and Buzz seemed to grow—no, it couldn't be. Is he growing arms? The spinning got faster, and I could hear Conall calling our names again and again—or was it an echo? Then, I lifted my wing; my feathers were skin, my wing a now a hand, and my beak a nose!

"Blossom, what is happening to us?" said Buzz.

"I don't know, but you don't look Lorikeet anymore—"

"Blossom—you're part Human, part Lori-Folk!"

The spinning stopped, and Conall untied the straps. I held out my Human Folk hands to him and said, "Conall, I'm a Lorifolk!"

He looked at me, stunned and said, "From Bird to Human but then—not quite, how is that possible?"

Buzz waved his arms and kicked his feet. "Lorikeet to Lorifolk in just one night. Oh, my!"

CHAPTER 20

ONE YEAR MORE

Before we go on, you need to know I'm Buzz, and I'm a Lorifolk. Don't worry; Blossom is—fine, well mostly, but is now a Lorifolk and asked me to tell this part of our story. Today is one year after that experiment, which partly changed us into Human Folk. It's the morning of the Human Folk entering what they call 'The Great War,' and I'm with Captain Lyle on his transport ship, Piare. I'm a cadet now, and we're taking on board a group of young Human Folk ordered to sail from Hobart to Port Huon to seize the merchant ship Oberon and arrest its German crew. It's all very strange. Oh, and I have a stopwatch now.

"Captain, we're ready to steam to Port Huon," I said to Lyle. He squinted and smiled back at me. As a cadet, I'm not supposed to use first names anymore.

"How many naval reservists do we have on board, Buzz—I mean, Cadet Buster?"

"Eleven, Captain. One of them slipped on the gangplank and dropped his rifle over the side, so we've stored all their guns below deck."

"These boys are as green as the water under this boat. We'll be docking with das Oberon by sunset."

"If I still had my beautiful wings, I'd be there by morning."

"You're an important part of my crew, Buzz, wings or not."

I wasn't so sure.

"Captain, I heard they've formed a group of flyers in Hobart."

"The Air Corps contingent? They fly in planes, Buzz—Buster—Cadet Buster."

"Yes, and planes have wings," I said.

He didn't reply and asked me to ring the ship's bell.

"Captain, what'll happen to the Oberon's crew after their ship is taken?"

"Port Huon was not the place for them to be once our King had declared war on their country. If our Imperial Forces force them from their ship, my guess is our German friends are in for an extended stay on Bruny Island, picking apples and pears."

"And their boat?"

"Renamed to serve as His Majesty's transport ship, probably in these very same waters."

"A gift from the people of Antwerp to the folk of Hobart?"

"You know, Buzz, I've watched the Oberon, year after year, steam up the river, all the way from Germany. She'd come in the summer and the spring with paper and iron and other things to be traded for our Tasmanian apples and tin. But each year, what I wait for, more than anything, as these hills fade a little more, is to happily pay for my new glasses from Germany. 'Von uns zu ihnen' is what they say in their language. 'From us to you.' The gift we trade, as friends will do."

Our sail to Port Huon took half a day. In the early afternoon, we heard a rumbling sound in the distance, and the boat pitched and rolled, so I rang the ship's bell, but it turned out to be nothing.

As sunset approached, I rang the ship's bell once more.

"The Oberon is in sight, Captain. The reservists are requesting their guns!"

Captain Lyle turned to me and very quietly said, "This is madness."

CHAPTER 21

THE POST OFFICE CLOCK TOWER, HOBART

"Spanner, please, Elena."

"One spanner, Professor Finlay. Now, can you please tell me why we are putting this marvellous piece of German engineering in the Clock Tower? And what does it have to do with that awful shaking last night?"

"It has a great deal to do with the tremor last night. I've been monitoring seismic activity for the last four years."

"As any good geologist, inventor, Antarctic explorer, and physicist must do."

"Well—yes, that's true—I have a few hats. Now, where was I?"

"You were about to say that this contraption on the floor is a seismograph. And that a seismograph records earthquakes and tremors."

"Oh, excellent, that's correct—though technically, Elena, the seismograph is recording the waves of energy caused by earthquakes and tremors that travel through the Earth."

"Mein fehler, my mistake, Professor. But why is it here in the Clock Tower?"

"Yesterday, I received a letter from the Hobart Meteorological Society inviting me to put it here. It was quite a surprise. A seismograph needs to be in a safe place, away from people who could bump it. The one in my workshop detected five tremors in 1910, two in 1911 and the big one in November last year."

"Yes, how could I forget? It was the night Blossom and Buzz helped you with your experiment, the night they became Lorifolk!"

"I'm so sorry; I feel so responsible. I'm researching why they changed the precise moment the tremor struck."

"Keep going, Conall. That's the best way for you to help them. I cannot imagine how difficult it's been for them to adjust to their new lives."

"You've been a superb guardian for Blossom, my love."

"As Lyle has for Buzz. But thank you. I worry that it's Buzz who seems to be having the most difficulty adjusting, especially not being able to fly anymore."

"Captain Lyle will look after his new sea cadet."

"I do hope it will help him settle. He's sweet, our Buzz."

"And Blossom has been blessed to have you as a mentor."

"Another compliment, Professor Finlay! Could all these clockworks be playing with that head of yours?"

"Oh—I just meant—Elena—"

"Yes, Conall?"

"If I were to pick a rock for you—I'd match your pale blue eyes with a stone so clear and cut so pure—"

"We've been friends for—how long has it been, Conall?"

"Aquamarine."

"Aquamarine, Conall?"

"The most beautiful eyes I've ever seen—oh, the seismograph, it's moving—another tremor."

"Another, right now?"

"Yes, the same intensity as the one at sunset last night."

"I thought that was thunder."

"It's definitely not thunder, and concerning that they're increasing in strength and frequency. Let me see, one final adjustment and—"

"Miss Meijer, you're now looking at the official Hobart Meteorological Society seismograph!"

"Hurrah! Goodness me, the Tower clockworks are so loud."

"What did you say?"

"I said, the Tower clockworks are so loud, Conall."

"This seismograph, Elena, will help research my theories. If you look outside that window—"

"What did you say?"

"Look west, towards Mount Kunanyi—I think there's a connection between these tremors and the Organ Pipes—On its eastern side!"

"Conall, why is there a Cat on the windowsill with a pocket watch around its neck?"

"What did you say, Elena? I can't hear you; the Clock Tower bell is so loud."

"I said, there's a Cat with—Let's go, I'll explain later."

CHAPTER 22

FITZPATRICK'S DEPARTMENT STORE, HOBART

Buzz told me he misses his beautiful wings now that we are Lorifolk. He talks a lot more nowadays, and sleeps in a Human Folk bed in a shack near Captain Lyle's boat at Sandy Bay.

I sleep in a nest of blankets at Elena's home in Claremont.

Since the experiment that went wrong, Elena has been very kind to me. I'm okay, mostly, just in the wrong body.

Today, Elena decided to take me shopping at Fitzpatrick's Store in Hobart because I needed, 'cheering up.'

The women behind the counters have their names pinned to their blouses. One of them, Mrs Harris, waved her hands as if they were wings and said to the other assistant that she saw a woman on the tram wearing an armband, with—

'WAR IS HORROR'

written on it, and they wouldn't be welcome in her store.

She turned to Elena and said,

"Miss Meijer, our Cremaline is the last word in new wool

blousing. It is far past anything produced in blouse fabrics. It has had just one season in London, and in that one season, the sales of Cremaline have beaten all blousing sale records. I'm sure someone as well-travelled as you, someone who speaks five languages fluently, would appreciate this quality. The price is two and nine per yard. Will you secure a length?"

Elena felt the cloth and said,

"Well, perhaps, but can we first—"

"Or, for your young Miss?" she said.

I asked her if she was talking to me. She looked at me from my Lorifolk head to my Lorifolk toe, but just kept talking to Elena.

"As I was saying, Miss Meijer, our very special line of paillette silks for blouses and evening wear in cream, vieux rose, navy, and pink? Only five and six."

"Well, my—" Elena gave me a funny look and patted my hand.

"My child isn't quite ready for—"

"Or perhaps our all wool cream delaines for blouses or dresses? An excellent washing fabric? Two and six a yard."

She kept chit-chatting about blouses and 'two and six a yard.'

I saw on a hat stand a large bonnet with bright-coloured feathers sticking out of it.

"Why do you have feathers in your hats?" I said.

"Or the plain Venetian cloth? We have all colours, only one shilling a yard."

"I asked you a question," I said, not as politely as Elena would.

Elena took me by the arm and, ever so sweetly, said,

"Excuse me, Mrs Harris, but we have another appointment."

"Or perhaps a nice heavy material for winter wear?"

"Feathers on a hat? That's ridiculous," I said.

Elena frowned at me.

"This Peacock boa, young Miss, is quite exquisite. And—the latest fashion statement!"

"Ridiculous!" I squawked at her.

She gave me the kind of smile Human Folk give, when they don't really mean it and said,

"Melbourne doesn't think so, Miss, nor Paris, I believe."

I squawked at her again.

"There's no need to be so rude," she snapped.

I pulled the feather from the hat.

"Get Mr Harris!" she shouted. "That will be four and six!"

I squawked again as Mr Harris arrived.

"Now, let's not make a scene, Miss," he said.

I told him I was not a Miss and that their hats were cruel and definitely not a fashion statement. But he said he'd call the constabulary if I didn't leave—at once.

Elena gently took me by the hand and whispered,

"We should go, Blossom, we'll miss our tram."

"What insolence," spat Mrs Harris.

And as we left, Mr Harris clapped his hands and said,

"Shoppers, we've plenty more bargains in the basement!"

CHAPTER 23

THE MASONIC HALL, HOBART

"You have five minutes at the lectern, Professor Finlay and no more. I suggest you stop shuffling your maps and drawings and get on with it."

"I, um— members of the Institute, distinguished Sirs, can I take just a fraction of your precious time?"

"Four minutes and thirty seconds, Professor Finlay."

"Ah, yes, four minutes and thirty seconds, thank you."

"It's now four minutes, precisely."

"I can assure you, Sirs, that my geological mapping of the Great Lake indicates the site is suitable. No, I take that back. It is highly suitable and excellent, in fact, for a hydroelectric scheme. A scheme that will—"

"Professor Finlay, I must interrupt. We're here to determine your suitability to remain a member of this Institute, not to hear another of your wild schemes."

"But, Sirs, please, this electric power development could—no, I mean can—will, harness the natural resources for our community benefit and—and yes, for industrial development in Tasmania—."

"Thank you, Professor Finlay. I think we have heard quite enough."

"If you would just cast your eyes over my engineering plans—I predict, when fully functional, it could—I mean, will have a capacity of seven megawatts of power."

"Goodbye, Professor Finlay; close the door behind you as you leave; there's a good man."

CHAPTER 24

MURRAY STREET, HOBART

"Those Masons are so 19th Century. Finlay, isn't it?"

"It's Professor Finlay, actually. How do you know my—? Is that your Cat?"

"You're a smart man, Mr Finlay! I could use someone like you."

"Do I know you? Mr—?"

"Gray, call me Gray."

"Mr Gray, and you're from the power company?"

"Not exactly, let's just say I'm—with the authorities."

"The authorities?"

"What do you know about cryptology, Professor?"

"What do I know about cryptology?"

"You're a smart guy, Mr Finlay. You've got it all—up here in your head, haven't you? How'd you like to share what's there with a fella like me?"

"With you? But I don't know—."

"Let's not play, Mr Finlay. You know cryptology?"

"I do, Mr Gray—but—"

"Of course, you do, Professor—and it's just Gray, by the way—cypher, codes, numbers, and rows, sure you do."

"I enjoy mathematics."

"You're a smart chap, Mr Finlay. You've been down South, haven't you, with your people and crew?"

"It's Professor, Mr—I mean Gray. Do you know Blossom and Buzz?"

"Ah—yeah. Yes, yes, yes—of course, I know them. You're a smart man, Mr Finlay. You've got it all up there in your head. Here's my card, don't think too hard! Got to go."

"But wait, Mr Gray, how will I know—?"

"Cheerio, Professor!"

CHAPTER 25
PORT HUON

"Lyle, my dear friend, what is their reason for detaining my crew? We are at Port Huon only to take on timber and then be on our way."

"Kapitan Joern, my friend, you and your crew are citizens of a country that, as of midnight last night, is at war with our Empire, and I'm sorry to tell you that the navy has commandeered the Oberon and your crew will be detained at Bruny Island."

"Falscher ort und falsche zeit, is it Lyle?"

"You are, indeed, my friend, in the wrong place at the wrong time. Cadet Buster here will escort you to Private Bridgewater of the Navy Reserves, who will give you your instructions."

"Hello, Kapitan, I'm Cadet Buster, and I'm sorry about this, Kapitan. You're on the wrong side of the world and the wrong side of midnight! This is Private Bridgewater."

"Thank you, Cadet. Kapitan, if you would please ah—um, tell your crew to collect their things and—um, disembark the

79

Oberon with my men—ah, straight away, please, sir, ah, Kapitan."

"Indeed, we will, Private, we will. Falscher ort und falsche zeit."

CHAPTER 26
THE WAR OFFICE

"Miss Meijer, thank you for popping in to meet with us today."

"Your telegram, Major, may have mentioned that I'm 'required' to meet with you at the War Office today."

"Yes, well, um—possibly. Tea? Get us some tea, will you, Sergeant?"

"No, thank you, Major."

"Oh, well, quite so—anyway, the fact is, Miss Meijer."

"Yes?"

"We Tasmanians, like the rest of the country, must play our part in this little adventure."

"It's a world war, Major, not an adventure."

"Ah, yes—and do you know, we Tasmanians must contribute—Sergeant, hand me that report. Let me see, ah yes, we Tasmanians must contribute two thousand recruits a month to the um—war effort."

"And why should it involve me?"

"Our little Birds have advised us—"

"Your little Birds?"

81

"A contact at the school where you teach music."

"Someone at my school gave the War Office my name. I don't think so."

"Well, no, not exactly—um—Sergeant?"

"The driver, Sir, the school bus driver."

"Thank you, Sergeant. The school bus driver, Miss Meijer. The driver understood—"

"Understood what, exactly, Major?"

"Well, perhaps he may have overheard through our little um—"

"Birds, perhaps, Major?"

"Ah, quite so. Well, the point is that you can speak many languages. Yes?"

"I see. And why would that interest you?"

"Well, you see, um— Sergeant?"

"The lady speaks fluent German, Sir."

"Why, of course, Miss Meijer, you speak German! Sprechen ze Deutsch!"

"I see."

"And, well, that would be immensely helpful, you see."

"Major, I have no intention of helping you or your war in any way. May I leave now?"

"Now, Miss Meijer, your Country needs you—"

"My Country is making a mistake."

"Well, um, nevertheless, you are required—"

"I'm required?"

"Yes, required to report, once again, to this Office, at, um —Sergeant?"

"Monday, Sir. Nine o'clock, Macquarie Street."

"Quite so, thank you, Sergeant, bright and early."

"And if I refuse?"

"Nine o'clock, Miss Meijer, and please bring with you Miss —um —Sergeant?"

"Miss Blossom, Sir."

"Yes, bring Miss Blossom along with you. We heard there was quite a fiasco at Fitzpatrick's store the other day. Such boldness for one so young."

"Absolutely not!"

"Miss Meijer, we would rather not have Miss Blossom typing away in a stuffy old office in Melbourne, would we? Better here, in Hobart, don't you think? Under your wing, so to speak?"

"I must protest, I—"

"Show Miss Meijer out, please, Sergeant. And close the door behind you and get me that cup of tea if you would."

"This way, please, Miss."

"You can step out from behind the curtain now, Mr Gray. Our guest has left."

"A rather feisty guest, Major."

"Do we have a problem brewing, Mr Gray?"

"We do, Major, and it's brewing more quickly than your tea. Worry not. My people will keep Miss Meijer and her Professor friend quite busy. In wartime, threats can come from any direction. Believe me, they'll have no time to spread their foolish opinions or silly theories. No time at all."

CHAPTER 27

THE VOICE OF THE ORGAN PIPES, KUNANYI

'And can you feel me breathing in
the land of ice and sea of white?
And do you hear me breathing out
the Organ Pipes of dolerite?
A stairway away waits for you
to enter below the land and sea.
An inner space of cogs and wheels,
of corridors and secrets revealed.

In the tallest column of dolerite,
not to the left or the right.
When a clock strikes six, five miles east,
I open a door within my midst.
Bring open minds, a coat, and light,
and I'll help you fight, the fight that's right'

CHAPTER 28
THE OLD HOUSE IN CLAREMONT

After taking the feather from that ridiculous hat, Elena asked me to spend some 'quiet time' at her home in Claremont. She read me from her prayer book, and we talked and had a good time.

Today is Friday, and we're hosting dinner for Buzz, Captain Lyle and Conall, who is already here. There's the door now. I'm so excited!

"Oh my, Buzz, what—"

"That's a sad face, Blossom. Were we meant to bring something?"

"Buster! You were meant to bring your senses! Elena, Conall, look! Buzz is in uniform!"

"A uniform?" said Elena.

"Is that an AFC uniform?" said Conall.

"Is that what this is? Funny, when I enlisted in the Australian Flying Corp, I didn't realise they'd give me a uniform!"

"Lyle, couldn't you stop him?" said Elena.

"I'm his guardian, not his father. He told me he was going to Sandy Bay for a swim."

"You can't swim," said Conall.

"I'm taking lessons at the swimming club."

I pulled at his jacket and said,

"You are taking that uniform back to where you got it—you're not even nineteen."

"Conall, you should have been there with me. They'd never seen a recruit do so well on the eye test before. Of course, they then forgot all about my age, which was fine because I have no idea how old I am in Human years anyway."

"Now listen, Buzz," said Conall, "Elena, Lyle and I, we're your friends and friends—"

"I'm not returning my uniform!"

"And why ever not?" asked Elena.

"Because they need flyers—"

"Conall, you must talk some sense into him, please," said Elena.

"Buzz, you know you can't fly—I mean, now you're unable to fly. I'm sorry my experiment altered both of your forms. I'm sure it's only temporary, and you will—"

"I'm nothing without my wings. Now I can be something."

"Buster, like me, you were hatched a Lorikeet and a Lorikeet—"

"Can fly! But now, thanks to someone who turned the knob before I could push the lever, I can't fly! Joining the Flying Corps is my one chance to soar across the skies again, and I'm not going to give that up because someone thinks the war is wrong!"

"Killing is wrong!" said Elena.

"I'll be searching for our wounded sons, defending the Empire."

"It's not your Empire," I said. "And they're not your sons. You, like me, are a Lorikeet!"

"I'm now a Lorifolk Blossom. And like you, I have Human skin, not feathers. That's my uniform."

"There's that word 'uniform' again," said Elena. "I'm tired of seeing the young of Hobart in military uniforms. It's all shiny buttons and straight rows, and it makes no sense; they're dominoes."

Buzz stretched his arms out like the wings of a plane and danced around the dining room table, singing about flying in a rare kind of air.

We left him prancing about and waited in the library until he'd settled and agreed to sit down for dinner.

Captain Lyle changed the conversation.

"Elena, I've braved the meals of our ship's cook all month. I've heard wonderful things about Blossom's apple pie."

"It's Elena's recipe," I replied. "Not only has she welcomed me into my new nest in Claremont and got me a job, but she has also shared her best recipes with me, using plants, nuts, and fruits."

"My mother's recipe," added Elena. "And you are an exceptionally clever young Lorifolk. I'm proud to be your guardian. Now, everyone, please sit. Blossom, will you give thanks, the one I taught you?"

"Of course. Now Buster—"

"Don't call me—"

"Buzz—please hold hands with Lyle and Conall. Conall with Elena. Elena and Lyle with me, and together, repeat what I say,

> *Friendships have no borders.*
> *Friendships have no bounds.*
> *Friendship is eternal.*

Friendship is profound."

And they did, and then I added, "All life is unique."

They repeated that, too.

Elena thanked me, and Lyle raised his glass and said, 'Here's to the cooks,' and Conall raised his glass and said, 'Here's to the guardians,' and Elena said, 'Let's eat,' and Buzz had three helpings of my apple pie.

After dinner, as we cleaned up, Conall told a strange story.

"I wished I had a guardian the other night. I met the oddest fellow who seemed to know everything about me."

"What fellow? Where were you?" asked Elena.

"Outside the Masonic Hall. His name was Mr Gray."

"Gray?" I said. "That name's oddly familiar—oh, my memory is so hazy now I'm a Lorifolk. What did he want?"

"What I knew about cryptology."

"Cryptography?" said Buzz.

"Cryp-tol-ogy. Numbers and codes. He seemed to know you and Blossom as well."

"We've never met him before," said Buzz. "Codes? Is he with the War Office, Conall? Recruiting the best and brightest?"

"The War Office, Buzz," said Elena, "Is not a polite dinner conversation. Blossom, please pass me the telegram on the sideboard."

"Everyone, I received this telegram the other day."

She read it aloud in a very official voice.

"Miss Meijer, you and Miss Blossom are required to report at nine am, Monday to the War Office, Macquarie Street, Hobart."

"Someone found out Elena is fluent in five languages," I said, "Including German."

"If I decline, we both could go to gaol."

"Can't you refuse on conscientious grounds?" said Lyle.

"Apparently, no!" replied Elena. "And meanwhile, our young go missing, feared lost."

"And Birds die to make a hat," I added.

Lyle shifted awkwardly in his chair.

"Well, I've betrayed my friend Joern and he's now in a goal on Bruny."

"And I ache for my beautiful wings," said Buzz.

We all were still and quiet for a while until Conall told Buzz he'd help find his wings, and Elena told me we'd make a feather-free hat.

We said our prayer again, and then Buzz asked for another slice of my apple pie, and Elena played the piano, and we all sang along, and we had a fine time until a distant rumbling sound made the glasses on the sideboard shake.

"What's that sound?" said Elena.

The house began to creak; a swirling, spinning began, like being caught on the edge of a storm. Things rotated and whirled, and it was all misty—

"Another tremor?" said Lyle.

"An earthquake?" said Elena.

"Neither," said Conall. "It's bigger and what I most feared, the Tempo Spirale is coming; its equation had eluded me."

"What is it, Connell?" shouted Elena.

"The continents are crashing in a time spiral."

Everything around us whirled faster, and the wind got louder and pushed the chairs over, and Conall's words about time spinning, continents crashing, and seas rising echoed about us but made no sense. And then there was a banging at the door, and I saw someone running, and then, in a far-off voice, Conall called—

"The equation is eating fear."

And he was gone, and Elena screamed, and I was scared.

CHAPTER 29

OUTSIDE THE WAR OFFICE

A bove the War Office's front steps on Hobart's main street is a sign stretched across the building.

YOUR COUNTRY NEEDS YOU!
RECRUITS WANTED. YOUR COUNTRY CALLS.

Elena and I stood behind a wooden table, which some military men had carried out after we'd reported in at nine am. They offered us tea and scones, but Elena said we were fasting for peace, so I didn't have any. A line of young men, boys mostly in civilian clothes, waited for us to take their particulars. Now and then, a soldier would tell the younger boys to stop slouching or to straighten their line, and a man in a suit would call out, 'Your country needs you!' through a rolled-up newspaper to any men passing by.

"Name?" I said to the next in line.

"King Edward," he said.

"Hilarious, young man," said Elena, "You're the eighth King who's enlisted this week."

I asked him to read and sign the declaration on the table and wait in another line, but Elena stopped him.

"How old are you?"

"Nineteen, Miss," he mumbled, trying not to look at her.

"Now, listen to me," said Elena, wagging her finger at him. "I didn't come down in the last shower, young man. Go back to school and stop wasting your life standing here."

He shuffled, then ran, disappearing around the corner.

Elena turned to me and whispered, "It's worrying enough that Conall is missing without these lads playing the fool with their lives."

"Lyle said he'll find him, and Buzz is frantic to help."

"Fingers crossed we hear something soon. I desperately miss him."

We returned to our list. I called out, "Next!" A young man took off his hat and stepped forward.

"Name?" I said, looking up at him.

"Gunther, Miss, that's a lovely bonnet, Miss."

"I'm not a—I mean, thank you, I—er—made it myself. Is that your name? Because—"

"It is Miss. My grandfather settled in Sorell Creek, north-west of here, fifty years ago."

A soldier nearby asked him if he spoke German. He said he did. The soldier then looked at me and said,

"Take this young lad to Mr Gray."

"Mr Gray?"

"Yes, Simeon Gray, wearing the suit over there. Look lively now, Miss."

"I can take the young man," said Elena, stepping out from behind the table.

I gave Elena a sideways look and led Gunther to the man wearing the suit.

"Excuse me, are you Mr Gray?"

He reminded me of someone.

"Yes, young lady? What is it?"

"I'm not a—I mean, the soldier over there asked me to bring Mr Gunther to you."

"Gunther? You speak German, I presume?"

"Yes, Sir."

"Mr Gunther's grandfather settled in Sorell Creek fifty years ago," I added.

"Thank you, Miss, that will be all."

"I'm not a—It's just that I was also wondering, Mr Gray, if you could help us find our missing friend."

"Many soldiers are missing. Give his name to the Major."

"But Professor Finlay is not a soldier."

Elena added, "He vanished the night of the earthquake, and we've not heard from him since."

"Well, that is something of a mystery. What a bother. When trying to find someone and time is of the essence, I go to where my face sees in every direction."

"But Mr Gray—"

"Sorry, must be off." He headed up the steps into the War Office and was gone. I turned to Elena and said,

"What did he mean, 'I go to where my face sees in every direction'?"

CHAPTER 30

AN AIRFIELD, HOBART SHOWGROUNDS

"I told you, Lyle. Flying a biplane is easier than sailing a yacht on the Derwent!"

"Don't be too confident, Buzz. It's only your second flight."

"Did you see me soaring across the showgrounds and how I landed precisely on the tarmac? If Blossom could see me now."

"Well done, very impressive. Now, switch off the motor, and we'll push her back into the hangar and have breakfast."

"I'll be doing what they call 'reconnaissance training' next week, so I need plenty of practice to search for Conall. Do you think he's lost off the West Coast?"

"There are no stranded ships off our waters."

"Conall said the Tempo Spirale—"

"Conall said something about fear. In wartime, fear is traded like apples. How can someone disappear like this? It seems to me there's something other than a blooming big earthquake at play here."

"I want to help, Lyle."

"You're our eyes and ears now, Buzz!"

"I'm ready! Fancy a quick flight to Bruny Island and back?"

"Bruny Island? Are you sure? I've never been in a plane before."

"I'm sure, and you said you have the mail for the crew of the Oberon?"

"Yeah, I do, but are you sure? I mean to fly in the sky in a plane—"

"It's wonderful, and there's no time like right now! Propeller, please, Captain! And then jump behind me into the cockpit."

"Well, here goes. I hope you know what you're doing, Buzz!"

"We're explorers, Lyle! Put those goggles on and hold on tight. We'll, 'be there in a jiffy,' as you Human Folk say!"

CHAPTER 31
THE INTERNMENT CAMP, BRUNY ISLAND

"Hello, Joern, apple picking, I see? One of the few benefits of internment, my friend?"

"Lyle, my friend, guten tag. Please help me down this ladder. That's enough apple-picking for today. Let me shake your hand, my friend. What a surprise! I wasn't expecting you."

"I wasn't expecting to see you, but Buzz needs flying practice and insisted I bring your crew their mail."

"Danke, danke, that is so kind of him, the flyer in the plane now, and you, please, sit my friend, sit here on this apple crate, and look here, it says on the side, 'Product of Tasmania,' wunderbar hey?"

"Danke, Joern."

"Please, Lyle, have an apple; I believe these fine apples would be bound for Germany if not for us visitors enjoying their exquisite taste."

"Danke Joern, they are, 'sehr gut,' as you say in Germany."

"Ja, excellent, Lyle. The authorities, they tell us, my crew are civilian detainees."

"These are strange times, Joern, strange times."

"Indeed, they are. Lyle, my friend, do you know, staring at these fine fruits all day, my mind wanders."

"How so?"

"The stories you share of your adventures in Antarctica. As I pick fruit all day, I wonder, is this the tree that grew the apple in the crate that the Lorikeet, Buzz, ate?"

"Ah, yes, the Hobart docks, your memory is good, Joern."

"I continue with my dream for you—the Captain saw the apple thief and, with your net, did a Lorikeet get. But Madam Elena heard the sweetest song and intervened. I wonder, Lyle, is this the tree that grew the apple in the crate my own Papa ate? Crispy and white, in a marketplace, in a Bremen port, a German bought. Is this the tree?"

"Well done, Joern, I applaud you!"

"Oh, what is that roar of a plane? It lands nearby?"

"That's my flight home!"

"Be well, my dear Hobart friend, be well."

"Goodbye, Joern, let's hope this mad folly will end soon."

CHAPTER 32
THE POST OFFICE CLOCK TOWER, HOBART

E lena and I raced towards the front steps of the Hobart General Post Office. The tower clock struck a quarter to six as its arched windows blinked in the setting sun and the copper roof gleamed.

"What a day it's been, Elena. Are you sure this is where Mr Gray meant?"

"I'm certain. This morning, he said, 'I go to where my face sees in every direction.' Look above you, Blossom."

I looked up at the Tower on the corner of the building.

"The Tower has a clock on every side."

"One central clock with four faces pointing north, south, east, and west. The entrance to the Tower is in the laneway. Conall placed a seismograph up there the other day."

"A seismograph?"

"I'll explain later."

The side door was locked; it had a sign on it—

NO CIVILIANS

I kicked it, really hard, and it burst open.

"Elena, what's a civilian?"

"Don't worry, Blossom. Quickly, up the stairway."

We hurried up endless flights of stairs; we could hear banging and crashing above us.

"Conall, are you up there?" shouted Elena.

"Elena, it's me, hurry!"

"Where are you?"

"I'm stuck in the clock mechanism."

"We've come to rescue you!" I cried.

As we arrived at the top of the stairs, we found Conall suspended on a platform above us, his coat caught in a cog within the clockworks, beside the Tower bell.

"Thank goodness!" said Conall, desperately tugging on his coat.

"When I heard you coming, I told the guard it was a foreign trap to steal the codes. He panicked, and in the confusion, I locked him in the room—over there. But as I tried to escape, I slipped and fell into these clockworks."

We heard thumping on the door.

"He has a radio; he'll be calling for help."

"We need to hurry then," said Elena, climbing the scaffolding towards him. "Conall, why was someone watching you?"

"It's Gray and his men."

"From the War Office? But he told us you're here. Why would he do that?"

"He did? What, when?"

"This morning. Blossom, throw me that rope. Conall, why would he do this to you?"

I threw the rope at them.

"It was the night of our dinner, when the Tempo Spirale hit."

Elena looped the rope over a beam suspended above the clock bell and swung one end towards him. "When you disappeared!"

Conall reached out to the rope with his foot. He missed.

"In all the confusion, Gray and his military police bundled me into a motorcar and locked me up here to work on code-breaking for the War Office."

"But why couldn't you tell us what you were doing?"

"Top secret! The codes were being sent by radio from Mount Wellington to the Clock Tower."

Elena swung the rope across again, and it landed in Conall's outstretched hand.

"Hold on, tight Conall!"

Elena swung from the rope, her weight pulling Conall free from the clockworks.

She gently lowered him to the scaffolding below. He hugged us both.

"My saviours!"

"But why did Gray keep you a prisoner?" I asked.

"I don't know. Once I'd deciphered the codes, he told the guard to keep me locked up, so I've been working on my theories about the Tempo Spirale."

"That's causing the tremors?" I said.

There was an engine noise coming from outside.

"A motorcar!" said Conall. "Gray's coming."

"Quickly, let's get out of here!" said Elena.

The Clock Tower bell rang. It was six o'clock.

We heard footsteps coming up the stairs. I turned to Conall.

"Is there another way out?"

Conall scanned the room.

"The clockface window, hurry."

Beside the cogs and wheels of the clock mechanism was a small arched window. We climbed out onto its ledge.

As I looked back, the military police stood at the top of the stairs. Mr Gray was with them. He pointed at us and screamed—

"Stop them!"

CHAPTER 33
KUNANYI AND THE CLOCK TOWER

As we carefully edged our way along the narrow ledge of the outer western Tower, the last rays of the setting sun shone on us, and the wind whistled about the massive black iron hands of its fourth clockface. We could hear Gray inside the Tower, spitting out orders to his military police. On the street below, the Pigeons pecked at whatever. To the west, the snow-covered peak of Mount Wellington and the rust-coloured dolerite columns of its Organ Pipes winked pink rays at us. How I wished to be there right now.

"Conall, what is the plan?" shouted Elena.

"We have a plan?" I thought aloud. My Lorifolk feet were hurting on the narrow edge.

"I'm thinking," shouted Conall.

Suddenly, the minute hand jumped forward, causing us to slip and lose balance. We quickly reached out and seized it to stop ourselves from falling.

"Think faster!" screamed Elena.

The shadow of a plane passed across the clock's face, changing its colour from pink to—suddenly, Gray stuck his head out the clock face window and, smiling oddly at us, said,

"Don't mind me. I'm just checking the time on the clock." He made a thing of looking at it and went on. "Oh, could you believe that, in ten minutes, it will be six thirty precisely, and unfortunately, that minute hand will hold you no more!"

"I deciphered the codes for you," said Conall. "Why this?"

"Why?" His smile melted. "Because people like you are dangerous!"

"People like you are evil," I shouted.

"Now, now, that's not appropriate behaviour for a young Miss." A Pigeon landed on his shoulder. "Get off, stupid Bird!"

He swatted the poor Pigeon, which squawked and tumbled, then regained flight and flew above him. I saw red, and my Lorifolk skin started to itch—a lot.

"Blossom, why is your hair changing colour?" shouted Elena.

"How dare you hit that poor Bird!" I yelled at Gray.

"The plane!" shouted Conall, as the minute hand ticked forward, unbalancing us again.

"Three minutes precisely!" heckled Gray.

"The plane?" said Elena. "You mean the plan? You have a plan?"

"No, the plane! Look, a plane! I'll send an S-O-S."

With his free hand, Conall reached into his vest and pointed the pocket watch at the sun.

"Please see us, please!"

The minute hand ticked forward once more. Elena lost her grip and, slipping over the edge, screamed—

"Conall, I'm—I'm falling—"

"Elena, no!" I screamed and jumped out to catch her hand.

As we both fell towards the street below, Conall, still hanging from the minute hand of the clock, cried out,

"No!"

In an instant, tiny Lorikeet wings sprouted from my shoulders.

Holding ever so tightly onto Elena's outstretched hand, I felt my wings, beating and flapping like a Humming-Bird, lift us past the clock face, towards the Tower's roof.

There was a tremendous roar of an engine; I turned to see the plane approaching with Lyle bravely standing on its wing, reaching out to Conall. He shouted—

"Jump to me, now!"

Conall leapt onto the plane's wing and landed safely in Lyle's outstretched arms.

Then, in a flip and a flap, my tiny wings carried me and Elena safely to the other wing of the plane.

Buzz, in the cockpit, hooted and cheered us and shouted,

"Hold on tight, everyone. It's going to get bumpy!"

He pitched the plane up and rolled it to the right, avoiding the Tower. As it clipped a few overhanging tiles on the roof, I heard Gray shout,

"I'll get you; I'll get all of you, mark my words—"

The Pigeon on the roof above him let go a poop, and as it slid down his face, I heard him moan, "I'm getting too old for this!"

"Oh, what a bother!" I called out to him as I held on to the plane strut, and we all laughed and hugged one another as the plane turned south.

Elena looked at me and said,

"Your wings, they're gone!"

I reached over each shoulder and felt small bumps underneath my Lorikeet skin on each side.

"Not completely, feel here—under my skin!"

Conall shouted—

"Everyone, we've no time to relax." He thumped the side of the cockpit and said—

"Buzz, to Mount Wellington."

The plane banked to the right.

"To the Organ Pipes!"

CHAPTER 34
THE ORGAN PIPES

In a flip and a flap, Buzz had landed his plane in a clearing not far from the Organ Pipes at Mount Wellington, and we all followed Conall along a bushy, snow-covered track to the bottom of its cliffs.

"You were a very brave co-pilot up there, Lyle," said Conall, giving him a big hug.

"It's good to be back on solid ground," Lyle replied. "These legs were made for land and sea, not walking the wings of a plane in the sky! Buzz's flying was amazing. I guess that's the Lorikeet coming out! And Blossom, your tiny wings appeared when Elena needed them most."

Elena looked at me with tears and cried, "Blossom, you saved my life. I'll never forget. Give me a big Lorikeet hug!"

As we hugged, Conall scraped the rust-coloured rock at our feet. "It's solid dolerite," he said, moving closer to the rocky pillar.

I scanned it from bottom to top. "Dolerite?"

"The Organ Pipes are made of dolerite! It's a type of rock

formed from boiling magma, deep underground. The same dolerite columns are in cliffs at Cape Denison."

"In Antarctica?" said Lyle.

"Exactly. The Tempo Spirale is moving the tectonic plates and forcing Earth's continents together."

"Conall, you're not making sense," said Elena.

"Well, that's nothing new," Buzz whispered to me, rather cheekily. "Blossom, what are you doing?"

"I'm massaging my wing bumps. I wonder, if I rub them, will they—?"

Conall held out his pocket watch and huddled us together. "Think of the Tempo Spirale as a mainspring, like the one inside my pocket watch or the mainspring in the Clock Tower clock."

"Don't remind me, please," said Elena.

"Right, of course, sorry Elena. Anyhow, as the tightly coiled mainspring unwinds, it releases power, which turns the gears that move the minute and hour hands."

"I see," said Lyle, not very convincingly, as he rubbed his chin. Conall turned to him.

"The Tempo Spirale is a much, much bigger mainspring. It moves continents, like moving hands on a clock."

"That clock must have a lot of hands," said Buzz.

"Well, figuratively yes, there would be seven for each continent," said Conall.

"So, the Tempo Spirale is a massive force moving Tasmania?"

"Yes, it has been, although very slowly, over millions of years. But now it's releasing force rapidly, causing the tremors."

"But why has it suddenly sped up?" said Elena.

"I'm not sure," said Conall.

"Perhaps the Earth is angry!"

"It has reason to be, with this horrible war," said Elena. "Conall, where is the Tempo Spirale? Is it underground?"

"I'm not exactly certain of the location of its source. I know all living things on Earth feel its force!"

"Mr Gray is a force. A force of evil." I said.

Lyle looked at me and said, "I agree with you, Blossom, but I don't believe Conall means that kind of force. More the force that creates the wind and tides."

"Like the Sun and the Moon," added Elena. "But Conall, why have you brought us here, to the Organ Pipes?"

"My theory is that each tremor we experience is the Tempo Spirale activating minerals in the dolerite of the Organ Pipes, creating an immense polar magnetic force pulling us towards the dolerite cliffs in Antarctica."

"Us?" said Elena.

"All of Tasmania and all the other continents of the Earth."

Lyle took off his cap and scratched his head. "Can we reset the Tempo Spirale back to its natural state?"

"We must!" said Conall. "The next tremor will be much, much stronger."

"We all can help," said Elena.

I raised my Lorifolk arm and added, "We'll ask the Lorikeets if they know anything. They can sense danger."

Buzz nodded. "We'll go straight to our eucalyptus tree and climb as high as possible." He jumped and, pointing east, said, "Look, signals coming from the Clock Tower."

"What do they say?" said Lyle, squinting to see the blinking lights.

Conall watched the flashing lights intently.

"The Ice Five are hot," said Conall. "It's code. We are the Ice Five. The five who went to Antarctica. I heard the guard say the Ice Five to Gray on the radio."

"And hot would mean we've escaped from him," added Lyle.

"He truly is an evil force," said Elena. "Gray's spies have been watching us all along. They were at my school and Fitzpatrick's Department Store."

"And when I visited Joern at the camp," said Lyle.

"Oh no!"

"What is it, Blossom?"

"I've just remembered. When the Aurora left for Antarctica, Gray was there, watching us."

"Was he now," said Lyle.

"He had a Cat. It had a pocket watch around its neck."

"Conall—the Cat," said Elena. "I saw that Cat at the Clock Tower when you installed the seismograph. Gray must have been there, spying on us!"

"And he was on an ice-flow, with a Lamplighter," I added.

"He's everywhere," said Buzz.

Conall gathered us in.

"We need to find the source of the Tempo Spirale and reset it. If we don't, these tremors will become catastrophic earthquakes, more destructive than ever before."

"The Earth is in danger," said Buzz.

"With Gray trying to stop us," added Elena.

"And a world fighting a deadly war," said Lyle.

I looked at my friends and said,

"Together, we must find the Tempo Spirale,
    unlock the key, release the spring
    and make the balance true!"

And we all replied,

"Together!"

CHAPTER 35
THE TREETOPS, TAROONA

A wild wind blew as Buzz and I stumbled along the narrow clifftop path to our Lorikeet home, high above the cliffs on the western side of the Derwent River. We helped each other climb up to a limb beside our nest in the hollow of the eucalyptus tree. The Derwent was raging below; it heaved, bumped, and frothed, the Dolphins and Penguins spun in its current, and the Sea Birds ignored them and whizzed downriver. Buzz stood on the branch and called out to a pair of Lorikeets rushing past us overhead.

"Hey, where are you going?"

No answer.

Buzz looked at me and, shaking his Lorifolk head, said, "Do we even make sense to them anymore?"

"Keep trying, Buzz, the world is in danger. Look, another pair of Lorikeets are coming. Climb up higher and try again."

He quickly made his way further up the trunk and wobbled out onto a thin branch that swayed in the gusting wind and called out again,

"Hey, Lorikeets, where are you going?"

The Lorikeets slowed on a thermal, rolled up and called back to him, "South, going south."

"Why, what's happening?" asked Buzz, balancing unsteadily on the branch.

In unison, the Lorikeets sang a song that whirled around us in the wild wind—

'Go to the tallest column of dolerite,
not to the left, nor to the right.'

"The Organ Pipes," I said. "You mean the Organ Pipes at Mount Wellington?"

Their song continued—

'When a clock strikes six, five miles east,
I open a door within my midst.'

"But wait," I said. "A door? There is no door."

They flew downriver and, from a distance, sang out to us—

'When a clock strikes six, five miles east,
I open a door within my midst.'

And then, they were gone.

"Conall," I said. "Buzz, we've got to tell Conall!"

CHAPTER 36

THE OLD HOUSE IN CLAREMONT

I listened for the three soft taps on the front door of Elena's home in Claremont.

"Password?" said Elena.

"Patagonicus," came the whispered reply.

Elena warily opened the front door. Conall rushed in.

"Quickly, it's not safe out there," he said, as Lyle and Buzz followed him inside.

"Thank goodness you made it," I said. "Were you seen?"

"Does the Cat next door count?" said Buzz.

"Supplies?" said Conall to Elena.

Elena pointed to five backpacks in the corridor.

"Everything on your list. Food, lamps and blankets."

Conall rummaged through each of the backpacks. "The binoculars?"

"Yes, Conall," replied Elena, producing the list. "Two pairs of binoculars, the compass, magnifying glass, small axe, water bottles and a flint."

"Our bicycles are out the back," I added.

Lyle placed a small green package in his pack. He then turned to us and said, "We follow the Lorikeets, then?"

Elena helped me with my pack and replied, "When a clock strikes six, five miles east—"

Together, Buzz and I replied, "I open a door within my midst."

Conall, throwing his pack over his shoulder, said, "We all agree. We ride to Mount Wellington tonight, in the cover of darkness, and arrive at the Organ Pipes just before sunrise at six am."

"We must be careful!" said Lyle. "It's dangerous. Gray will come for us."

"Just let him try!" said Buzz.

And we formed into a circle, held hands, and together said,

'Friendships have no borders.
Friendships have no bounds.
Friends come back tomorrow.
Friends are all around.'

CHAPTER 37
THE ORGAN PIPES

We rode all night in the cold. Our lamps lit our way in the heavy fog along the steep road to Mount Wellington, and as the sun began to rise, we made our way down the snowy track to the Organ Pipes, to the tallest dolerite column, not to the left, nor to the right.

In the distance, the Clock Tower bell rang out. It struck six o'clock.

There was a flash and a deep rumbling sound. Ever so slowly, at the bottom of the tallest column, a gold and silver door emerged from within the rock. Gradually, it partly opened, releasing a blinding light.

PART THREE
BLOSSOM AND BUZZ AND THE STAIRWAY AWAY

CHAPTER 38
THE STAIRWAY AWAY

Carrying our heavy packs, we carefully entered through the door into a long cave lit by a gold and blue glow. We slowly stepped down a very steep stairway for what seemed to be many long hours, finally reaching a long passageway.

"I'm so hungry," said Buzz. "What I would give for a crisp white apple now."

"What I would give for a rest from you talking about being hungry," I told him.

"Escaping from Mr Gray is hungry work," he replied, dropping his pack down.

"Finding and resetting the Tempo Spirale will be even harder work," said Conall.

"To stop the world's continents colliding is worthy work," said Elena.

Lyle lowered his pack and said, "Let's rest for a moment. We've been awake all day and night since we left Claremont. Elena, Conall, put your packs down."

We sat and took off our packs. Lyle then said,

"Well, I have a gift for you all!"

"A gift?" said Elena, rubbing her tired legs.

From his pack, Lyle pulled out a package wrapped in green cloth.

"Before we left, one of my crew made me a set of these in Tasmanian tin!" He held up a shiny pipe. "It was a gift."

"Tin whistles!" said Conall.

Lyle blew a note from the whistle that echoed down the passageway.

"Each will play one note only. I only wanted five, but he insisted on making a complete set of seven—one for each note from A to G."

"Together in harmony!" I said.

"Correct," replied Lyle, and he placed the whistle around my Lorifolk neck and said,

"B is for Blossom!"

"Perfect, thank you, Lyle."

"And C is for—"

"That must be Conall? Thank you, Captain Dalzell."

"My pleasure, Conall, and—D is for Dalzell; this is mine. And so, the E must be for our mainsail; here you are, Elena."

"It is divine, Lyle."

"And F? Who could F be but my young friend here? Buzz, my friend, thank you for always looking out for me."

"Always, Captain Dalzell," said Buzz, slapping Lyle on the shoulder.

"Thank you, Buster."

"We still have the A and G whistles, though," said Elena.

"We do indeed," said Lyle.

As I played with my whistle, wondering about the two orphaned notes, a sudden rush of wind approached us.

"Listen!" said Conall, rising to his feet. "Do you hear that? It sounded like a Cat."

"It's only the wind, Conall," said Lyle.

"But a wind in here? There must be another entrance then."

"Or a way out?" said Buzz.

We quickly gathered our packs as the wind became stronger and the gold and blue glow faded to darkness. As we fumbled in our packs for our lamps, an eerie hum grew louder, and pictures of people appeared on the tunnel walls.

"Oh, my Lord," said Elena, as faces of all shapes, colours, and ages passed by.

"Who are they?" said Buzz, amazed. The hum echoed about the passageway, and a voice spoke—

> *'Your generation stains the sky.*
> *Your angry leaders hate and lie.*
> *A grim future is beckoning,*
> *without a profound reckoning.'*

The gold and blue glow returned as the faces faded away.

"A grim future?" I said.

"We've left a world at war," said Elena.

"And a clashing of continents," said Buzz.

"Who took their photographs?" said Lyle.

"And how?" said Conall. "The camera was invented only sixty years ago. Some of those people lived thousands of years ago."

There was a flash and a deep rumbling sound, and a gold and silver door emerged from within the rock ahead. Gradually, it opened, releasing a blinding light.

We carefully stepped through into an open field of green, circled by misty blue mountains. Lorikeets flew by.

I scanned the horizon and said,

"Look, over there, beyond the mist. Is it a tower?"

"It is, with a turret clock on its steeple," said Conall.

My wing buds tingled as we followed a winding path to a gentle stream.

"This place seems strangely familiar," said Buzz.

"I've the same feeling," said Lyle.

Buzz waded across the stream.

"This water is freezing!"

"I don't want to alarm anyone, but we are being watched," said Conall.

"Ahead, across the stream, behind that tree," said Elena.

"It is an inquisitive kind of look," I replied.

A young Human Folk in a gold and blue cape, carrying a long stick with a blue Orb on top, stepped out from behind the tree.

"Welcome, strangers. What brings you to my land?"

An eyeglass contraption was strapped to their side, each eyepiece steadily rotating gears, cogs, and levers. The blue Orb began to glow.

"My name is Blossom, and these are my friends. What is your name?"

"A child of the Lorikeet does not know who I am? How curious? I am Amari, the apprentice to the Vistarian."

Amari held up the thing strapped to her side, pointed to the tower and said,

"And the keeper of the Vistoculos."

Buzz stepped forward and replied, "Who is the Vistari— and how do you know?"

I gave him a sharp look and, smiling at the stranger, said, "We're all so pleased to meet you, Amari. This is Buzz—." I nudged him to step forward.

"Hello—um—Amari."

Amari gave him a little bow and said,

"Also, a child of the Lorikeet."

"And Elena."

"Hello, Amari; lovely to meet you."

"The singer," Amari said, again with a polite bow.

"And Captain Lyle."

Lyle reached out to shake Amari's hand, dropping one of his spare whistles. "Good Morning, young er—"

"The navigator," said Amari, picking up the whistle and handing it back to him.

"And—"

Conall stepped forward. Amari smiled, pointing to his vest pocket.

"The Time-Tinker, you have a timepiece near your heart."

"I do," said Conall with a grin, then glanced at his pocket watch. "My name is Conall."

"Amari, have we met before?" I asked.

"In a way—but you have not answered my question. What brings you here?"

"The Lorikeets, from—" I wasn't sure which direction was home. "From, where we all come from, told us to go to the Organ Pipes, and so we did, and when the clock struck six, a golden door opened—"

"And we went through it," said Elena.

"And followed a long passage past all the faces," added Lyle.

"And here we are," said Buzz with a smile. "Amari, where exactly are we?"

Amari smiled back at him. "Do you not recognise your home? You have just crossed the Derwent River."

"This stream is the Derwent?" said Buzz.

"A younger Derwent, but the Derwent all the same."

Conall put his pack down beside the stream.

"Amari, what year are we in? What time—"

"Time? Time is only a concept, Conall. You know that better than most."

I pointed to the strange tower in the distance and said, "Amari, you're the apprentice to the Vistarian. Do they live in that Tower?"

"The Vistarian is master of this Vistoculos, but he's old, and his hands tremble."

Conall looked at the rotating gears, cogs, and levers of the Vistoculos and said,

"Ancient text mentions the Vistarian. I thought it was folklore."

"Lorifolk history is not folklore," Amari replied. "The Vistarian must watch the horizon."

"The horizon, why?" said Elena.

"To protect us."

"Us?"

"The Florna, all living things—"

Overhead, a flock of Lorikeets screeched as a swarm of blue insects approached us. Amari's Orb began to glow, and my wing buds tingled.

"What is it, Amari?" said Conall.

"Sound Snatchers!"

The insects swarmed around Elena, who slumped to the ground and sang out high notes and trills in a kind of trance.

"Quickly, Time Tinker, hold the singer's mouth tightly closed," said Amari to Conall.

"Her mouth?"

Amari raised the Orb above her. "Do it now, or her voice will be stolen forever!"

As Elena shook uncontrollably, Conall and Lyle struggled to cover her mouth with their hands as she seemed to rise off the ground out of their reach.

Buzz wrapped his arms around me.

Amari wove the glowing Orb around us and called out—

"Not this day.
Return to your place, your time and space.
Tell your Maker that Amari won't forsake the
    singer.
Now, leave them be, let them be free.
Leave now!"

Elena slumped into Conall's arms, alive but exhausted.
Amari lowered the Orb and said,
"Your friend, the singer, must rest. We go to the Tower of the Vistarian."

CHAPTER 39

A NEW, OLD LAND

Together, we carried Elena along winding paths through a valley of yellow and crimson flowers and stands of cherry and walnut trees. Now and then, Amari would stop and hold the Orb up to the sky as if it were guiding her.

Finally, we arrived at the Tower of the Vistarian. Lyle said it appeared to be built of iron and rivets, like the black steam boiler below the deck of the Aurora.

As we made our way up the steps to its enormous, red, wooden door, Amari waved the Orb once again, and an unusual little being opened it and, smiling, said,

"Welcome, voyagers, to the Master's home."

"Onré, we encountered the Sound Snatchers," said Amari, placing the Vistoculos carefully on a table. "Our guests need food and rest. I will wake the Vistarian."

"Come, come. Sound Snatchers, you say? Oh my, oh my— the Vistarian will be so—."

Onré's voice trailed off as he led us along a corridor

crammed with odd symbols and strange signs to a library of books stacked from floor to ceiling along every wall.

Conall gently placed Elena on the settee and held her. Onré opened a side cupboard nearby to reveal platters of curious foods. There were walnuts, cherries, apples, and flowers in every rainbow colour. He then pushed a little cart of tall bottles of bubbling blue water to us and gave Buzz and me a wink and a nod to help ourselves. I sipped the bubbly blue water, which reminded me of winter and eucalyptus.

Lyle removed his glasses and examined the brass eyeglass contraption near a large bay window that overlooked a balcony leading to a distant horizon of blue mountains, shrouded in mist. For a moment, I thought I saw a great Blue Whale drifting across the cloudy sky, and I set the bubbly blue water down.

"This telescope is a thing of rare beauty. I've never seen anything like it before."

"It is a centuries-old Vistoculos," said Onré, offering drinks to Elena and Conall.

Amari wheeled the Vistarian into the library in an old wooden chair. The Vistarian, dressed in blue and gold robes and thick gold spectacles, seemed very old and almost blind. Onré placed a drink in the Vistarian's bent and twisted hand. We all stood, including Elena, who was awake but quite weak.

The Vistarian pointed his crooked finger at the ancient Vistoculos near the bay window and then, pointing to Lyle, said, "That was my first Vistoculos, given to me by the old Vistarian when I was seven. Please drink, eat, and rest. You are our guests and very welcome."

Buzz clumsily sat near the bookshelf, bumping into a thick book that fell to the floor. It gently floated back to its spot on the shelf. I whispered to Buzz not to drink too much. He turned to the Vistarian, bowed awkwardly and said, "We are on a quest. We've come from our time to find the Tempo Spirale and reset its key."

The Vistarian nodded to him and smiled. I then stood and bowed to him as well.

"My name is Blossom, and this is Buzz. We are Lorik—"

"Lorifolk," interrupted Buzz. I gave Buzz a stare and continued with the introductions.

"These are our friends: Professor Conall Finlay, Elena Meijer and Captain Lyle Dalzell, who are Human Folk."

"Indeed, they are, young Lorifolk. Indeed, they are."

He chuckled, then coughed, and Onré helped him drink.

He continued,

"And your quest is noble. Now, let me introduce myself. I am the Vistarian and have worked the horizon since childhood. I ride the early morning swells, I watch the horizon breathe, and I look for changes in the air. I mend holes, then and now, far and near."

He coughed again, and Amari helped him with his drink.

"But I am old and weary now with my powers fading."

He gently patted Amari's hand.

"Amari is our future and has displayed considerable talent as Keeper of the Vistoculos."

"Keeper of the Vistoculos?" said Buzz.

"I guard it, ready for its Master," said Amari, gesturing to the Vistarian. "It protects us. The Vistarian is one of the great custodians of time and also my mentor."

He smiled at Amari.

"Perhaps. However, I cannot ignore that The Gray has caused much pain and suffering on my watch."

He pointed a crooked finger at us and added, "And in your place and time."

"The Gray?" said Lyle.

"You may know him by another name," said the Vistarian. "He moves through time and place. He seeks to control others."

Elena put her drink down, straightened up and said, "Do you mean, 'Mr Gray,' from our century?"

"We may," said the Vistarian. He waved his wrinkled hand at Onré.

"But such discussion is for another time. Onré, our guests have experienced the aural charms of the Sound Snatchers. That is enough adventure for one day. Have you—?"

Onré pointed to a stairway leading to a loft above the bay window.

"Your rooms are ready; please come this way."

As we readied to follow Onré, the Vistarian gave a tiny wave to Lyle and whispered,

"Captain Lyle, may I have a moment of your time, please?"

"Why, of course, Sir," said Lyle, somewhat surprised.

CHAPTER 40

THE TOWER OF THE VISTARIAN

Conall, Elena, Buzz, and I followed Onré up the stairs to a loft above the library. It opened to a balcony that encircled the Tower. Each guest room faced a different direction: the sea, the valley, the forest, or the mountains. Buzz and I gazed at our view. Above us, stars shimmered in the evening sky.

"Look, Buzz, those trees over there are just like Taroona."

"But that stream we waded across? How could it be the Derwent?"

"Amari did say, 'Time is only a concept,' Buzz."

"And Blue Whales in the sky?" said Buzz, pointing above us to a Whale floating by, hiding a group of twinkling stars.

"And Mr Gray is 'The Gray,' how can that be?" I replied as the Whale drifted away.

"And Sound Snatchers?" said Buzz. "They had better not try and steal my voice."

"Thanks for looking out for me—when they swarmed."

"You're welcome, Blossom. It's what friends do."

"Lyle was right. F for a friend, like the whistle around your neck."

I patted Buzz on the shoulder. He shuffled and said,

"So, Amari is a Lorifolk, like us?"

"I'm not exactly sure what I am anymore," I replied.

A comet spiralled across the sky.

"Let's get some rest, Blossom. It's been a long day."

"I might sleep out here tonight," I said. "I can make a fine nest with a blanket."

"Goodnight, Blossom."

"Night, Buzz."

CHAPTER 41

THE LIBRARY

As I lay in my nest, a pod of Blue Whales gracefully drifted above me, their sparkling eyes replacing the stars they hid. How could I sleep? I looked over the balcony at the faint outline of mountains on the horizon. In the stillness, I thought about the Vistarian mending holes in the horizon.

I could hear his frail voice and realised I must be above the Library. I listened—.

"Look at the old Vistoculos more closely, Captain. Do you see the engraving on it?"

"Oh, on its side, yes, it reads—let me see—

Seven horizons, Seven seas,
Seven planets, the Seven keys."

"Excellent, Captain, and below that, it reads,

Seven heavens, Seven notes,
Seven colours, Seven quotes"

"Oh, yes—so it does."

"Your necklace. It is unusual. Is it a gift?"

"The whistle? Oh—it's a birthday gift from one of my crew."

"Could today be your birthday, Captain?"

"Well, yes—but how did you know? I didn't mention it to the others. It seemed unimportant, what with everything that has happened to us today."

"Reaching four sevens is far from unimportant, Captain Lyle Dalzell."

"Why yes, but how—?"

"One's twenty-eighth birthday is very significant in this place and time."

"How so?"

"I became the Vistarian as a young boy, not because I was in any way gifted but because, on the day the old Vistarian died in my village, I was the only one whose age was a multiple of seven, and so I became the new master of the Vistoculos."

"Seven?"

"Yes, come sit down. Indulge me, Captain Lyle, navigator of the sea."

"Thank you. I've sailed the seven seas since I was a boy."

"But can you navigate your most challenging voyage?"

"I'm not sure I understand."

"Even I, almost blind, can make out you awkwardly reaching for your spectacles. You strain to see the writing on the old Vistoculos. Your sight has become elusive, has it not?"

"I do wear spectacles, but Buzz helps me."

"The young Lorifolk helps you, do they? Well, I need you to help me."

"Help you? How?"

"My 'telescope,' as you call it."

"Your Vistoculos?"

"It is yours."

"I'm sorry?"

"It is yours now; you, navigator, are twenty-four times seven!"

"But Amari is your apprentice. It belongs to—"

"Amari is thirteen, Captain Lyle, and needs a mentor until their fourteenth year."

"I understand it's a multiple of seven, but—you are the Vistarian, and my eyesight—"

"The Vistoculos will be your eyes, Captain."

"But our journey here—"

"Your journey ends here if we cannot stop The Gray."

"Of course I want to help, but—"

"I am dying, Lyle."

"No—"

"Yes. It's time for me to pause this life. To go to a different time. No more riding swells in the early hours and mending holes with faded powers. I've finished my test and now offer this quest to someone kind and trustworthy. The Vistarian is you."

"Sir, sir, are you alright? Can you hear me?"

"Amari, Onré, come. The Vistarian has died!"

CHAPTER 42

THE INVESTITURE

L yle, dressed in silver and blue robes, stood on the grand balcony at the head of the coffin of the Vistarian. He looked different, and I realised he wasn't wearing his much-loved German spectacles. Amari, beside him, in flowing green and gold, held the Vistoculos in her right hand. Onré gently placed the Vistarian's first Vistoculos, given to him when only seven, upon the coffin.

Buzz and I, Elena and Conall, and countless Birds, Blue Whales and other Creatures watched Amari raise the Vistoculos above Lyle's head and speak,

"Do you, Captain Lyle Dalzell, who will, in time, come from this land, accept the responsibilities of the Vistarian to master the Vistoculos and protect our lands and Florna?"

"I accept these duties until you, Amari, Keeper of the Vistoculos, come of age."

"Then, by the authority bestowed upon me as Apprentice to our beloved brother, Constantijn van Baerle, who now sleeps beside us, announce you, Vistarian and the Master of the Vistoculos."

Amari placed the Vistoculos on Lyle's head. Each eyepiece of the strange contraption swelled, and its gears, cogs, and levers clicked and whirled.

Onré stepped forward and presented the Orb to Amari, who, turning to the gathering, held it above her head and called out,

"All welcome, the Vistarian!"

And we all replied,

"The Vistarian!"

And we cheered the new Master of the Vistoculos.

CHAPTER 43
THE OLD DERWENT

After the ceremony and the party that followed it, Onré escorted our new Vistarian on a tour of the Tower to explain their official duties and responsibilities. Meanwhile, Amari took Buzz, Elena, Conall, and me for a walk in the lush grounds of the outer Tower. Above us, the Blue Whales gently drifted across the sky, their long, glossy bodies peacefully rolling as their limp flippers trailed beneath them.

We stopped to admire many streams and grottos filled with water lilies, blooms and croaking Frogs, and as we strolled past a stand of bushy green trees with golden trunks, surprised Birds would scatter from their hollows, leaving a rainbow trail across the air as they flew from tree to tree.

Amari told us we were safe here but still carried the blue Orb and, as Keeper, the Vistoculos.

Buzz and I arrived with Amari at the bank of the ancient Derwent River, where a giant brass clock had been erected on a rocky point. Amari told us it was an ancient timepiece, a 'Turret Clock,' and two others had been found in the valley.

"The mechanism has been broken all summer," she said as we scrambled over the rocks to be closer. "The minute hand bounces back and forth every second."

"Don't worry, Amari," I replied. "Conall will know how to repair it."

"He's clever," said Buzz. "Once, he exploded Blossom into the sky on a firestick—here they come now."

Conall and Elena arrived and paused to rest on the rocks. "What a remarkable land this is," said Elena. "You are truly blessed to live here."

"How are you feeling, Elena?" asked Amari.

"What else could I be feeling in this place but wonderful? I'm quite recovered from those horrid Sound Snatchers."

Conall gave Elena a little hug and then turned his attention to the giant clock.

"A Turret Clock, here in the wilderness? How curious."

"The minute hand is stuck, Conall," said Buzz. "How do we fix it?"

Conall examined it more closely. "It is of incredible quality. Do we have a key, Amari?"

Buzz blew his whistle. "How about an F major?"

I laughed and then blew my whistle. "Or a B major?"

Conall chuckled, "Not that kind of key, a key to wind its mechanism."

Amari stepped up to the pedestal on which it was mounted. "There isn't one that I know of, but when you open this little door here, look, there's the sign of the Florna."

Behind the door was an oddly shaped handprint carved into a wooden plate.

"Yes, of course, it's the sign of the Florna," said Buzz rather knowingly. He turned to Amari and, smiling, said, "Amari, what is the sign of the Flora?"

"It's a sign of harmony between creatures."

"In our time," said Conall. "We show a red crescent or cross as a sign of aiding the suffering."

"Our sign is similar. Could this be the clock's key?"

"It's an odd-shaped handprint," I said. "It has six fingers."

"Yes, with two thumbs," said Buzz.

Conall placed his hand into the imprint. "Fascinating." He turned to Elena. "Elena, hold up your left hand, my love, with your palm facing you. Now, if I place my right-hand palm on the back of your hand—"

"The sign of the Florna," said Amari. "See, the thumbs stick out on each side."

"Buzz, place your left hand in the imprint in the mechanism."

"I'm not going to regret this, am I, Conall? We do have a history of a couple of minor experiments, taking an—"

"Unexpected turn?" I replied.

"I can assure you both, it's perfectly safe."

Buzz placed his hand on the handprint. "It feels soft, like feathers."

"Amari, please place your right hand over Buzz's left hand."

As Amari placed their hand over Buzz's, the timepiece began to chime, and the minute hand rapidly swept around the clock face.

"Oh my, it's working!" said Elena.

"I guess it has some time to make up," said Buzz with a twitter.

As the chime continued, we noticed Amari's Orb was glowing, and a distant bell rang. Amari seemed frightened and said,

"Something's wrong. That's the Tower bell. Come on, let's make our way back to the Vistarian."

"Amari, look," I said, pointing back to the river. The clock's spinning hands had become a spiral blur, and the water around it swirled, foamed, and drowned the platform we stood on moments earlier.

"Hurry," said Amari.

CHAPTER 44
THE GRAY HAS A DREAM

Amari bustled us to the safety of the Tower. Once inside, we followed Onré to the grand balcony where our new Vistarian, Lyle, dressed in gold and silver, stood high on a platform that slowly turned north to east and south to west. As he raised his hands to the Vistoculos on his head, its gears, cogs, and levers clicked and whirled, and each eyepiece swelled.

"He's here; Gray is in this time and close, near the horizon, asleep, but he dreams—"

> *'I see numbers in a nightmare quark,*
> *math chaos multiplying, in the dark.*
> *Digits consume me, and particles flash.*
> *I dream dangerously towards a crash.*
>
> *So, I arrange my life within a box*
> *of three dimensions and double locks.*
> *Don't come to me with an extended hand*

to change the world with some grand plan.
Change is perilous, unsafe, and extreme.
Why shift the chaos outside a dream?
With equal sides and double locks,
I live my life within a box.

The trouble brewing, although my doing,
is aimed to keep your ideas at bay.
Within my walls, I can't unravel and wobble—no
    Ice 5 meddling dimensional squabble.

Within three dimensions and double locks,
I live my life within a box.

There's an Organon to play not far from here,
but its keys freeze when I appear.
Locked out of my control or demand
to manipulate time on command.
I walk there nightly in the dream
and wake to music never seen.

Is sleep another maze in time?
To number-count, rank, define?

Or is it a world to foresee the coming,
shape the future, and evolve my cunning?
With equal sides and double locks,
I live my life within a box.'

Lyle lowered his hands from the Vistoculos and turned to
Amari, who said,
    "This flood is all part of The Gray's plan."

She pointed to the Derwent River in the distance.

"The Derwent's five fathoms deep and rising."

"Look below," said Lyle.

"The gardens around the Tower are already underwater."

"Amari, how can we get closer to the Derwent?"

CHAPTER 45
THE BLUE WHALES HELP US

With the help of a Blue Whale drifting overhead, Buzz and Amari, suspended by ropes from the Whale's long fins, floated above us.

"Lyle, there's an old wooden ketch downstream," shouted Buzz.

"I hope the Whale doesn't decide to take a swim in the Derwent," I said to Elena.

"Amari assured me our Whale friend is most reliable," said Conall.

"I do hope so," said Elena. "Are you ready, Blossom? Here comes your rope."

I jumped onto the rope and joined Amari and Buzz.

"Buzz, how big is the boat?" shouted Lyle.

"She's a seventy-footer, Captain," shouted Buzz.

"A seventy-footer, Vistarian," added Amari, scowling at Buzz.

"A seventy-footer, Vistarian—Lyle," shouted Buzz.

I looked at them both. "Both of you, stop it, please. This has been happening since Lyle—since the Vistarian became the Vistarian."

"Buzz needs to show some respect for his new role, that's all," said Amari.

"I'll have you know—I've known the Captain for—"

I swung my rope across to Buzz. "Buzz, that's enough!"

"They started it," said Buzz.

"I did not," said Amari.

"Amari," shouted Lyle. "Ask your Whale friend to drift closer to the boat. I'm sure it's the Acielle. She was built in Hobart a few years ago. Though how that can be—"

"I'll sail her to the Tower Captain!" shouted Buzz.

"I will, Vistarian," shouted Amari.

"Hurry, Amari," called Elena. "The boat's in a whirlpool."

The Whale rolled towards the swollen Derwent River and the spinning sailboat.

"Blossom, Buzz, are we ready to jump?" called Amari.

Buzz leapt and, as he fell towards its deck, cried, "I'm ready!"

"Ready, Blossom?" said Amari.

"Ready as I will ever be! One, two, three—jump!"

CHAPTER 46
THE DERWENT SKIRMISH

As we jumped from the ropes onto the deck of the Acielle, our Whale friend winked at us before gently sliding into the Derwent's angry waters.

In a flip and a flap, Buzz took the wheel and brought the spinning ketch under control. As the Lorikeets squawked at us from the nearby trees along the riverbank, Buzz steered the boat upriver towards the Vistarian's Tower.

"What is that up ahead?" called Buzz.

About a boat's length ahead of us, something—maybe a Human Folk—danced like a Chicken on the turret clock we'd visited earlier, now nearly submerged by the swollen Derwent River.

"There's trouble brewing," said Amari, her hands tightly clutching the glowing Orb. "Sound Snatchers are swarming around whoever that is, but they're not bothered."

"What in the world, Blossom! Look, it's him!" shouted Buzz.

I stared at the dancing figure, unable to believe my eyes— but it was him! My Lorifolk skin tingled, and I called out,

"So, you couldn't resist us, Mr Gray, or is it 'The Gray' now? I was hoping you were still trapped at the Hobart Clock Tower, all covered in pigeon poop!"

He smiled a silly, Human Folk smile and replied,

"Oh, very clever, sticks and stones! You've all arrived just in time for the party. Well, when I say party, some might refer to it as a catastrophic flood, destroying everything in its wake, but not me. No, it's just a little soirée to teach you meddlesome Lorifolk et al. a huge lesson!"

Amari pointed the Orb at Mr Gray and shouted, "I'd like to see you try Gray!"

"It's The Gray, actually, and I'd appreciate a bit more civility from you, Amari. Also, don't point that at me unless you want another visit from my invasive species."

He waved above to the Sound Snatchers. "Hello, chums!" He smiled at me, a sickly-sweet smile and said, "How's your multi-lingual operatic friend again? Elena, is it? A little quieter nowadays, I presume?"

Buzz moved our ketch closer. "Get him!" he shouted.

"Not flying today, Buster? What was it? 'In the tallest column of dolerite, not to the left, nor to the right.' I played hopscotch at the Organ Pipes long before your species hatched!"

"You knew the Stairway Away was there?" said Buzz.

Gray spun on the Turret Clock, watching every turn of the boat.

"Oh yes, my wingless friend, of course I did. You don't think I was foolish enough to be stumped by that interfering Time Tinker, friend of yours, do you? How dare he reset my clock!"

"We're trying to stop the tremors and quakes," I said.

"Oh, that's rich," scoffed the Gray. "Creating chaos in 1914. You try resetting the Tempo Spirale. It has controlled time over millennia! It's not easy, I'll let you know! A trivial wobble now and then is to be expected."

Like an Eagle, I watched him prancing on the clock. My wing buds tingled.

"Why, Gray? Why all this madness?"

"I wouldn't go there if I were you, Lorikeet."

"But what does it achieve?"

"I don't need the Ice Five, the Vistarian, or the Keeper here meddling inside my walls."

"Your walls? This is everyone's place and time, and it doesn't belong to you."

"Oh, you are so wrong. Once I've solved the sonata that's locked the Tempo Spirale and unleashed its awesome power, all time and all place will be controlled by yours truly to play with. Who knows what I could get up to controlling spiral time?"

"Why I could be—"

Shielded by the swarm of Sound Snatchers, he jumped from the clock onto the boom of the Acielle.

"Here!" he shouted.

Then swung over to the port side and cried,

"Or here!"

Then leapt back to the Tower Clock and shrieked,

"Or in infinite time and space!"

He waved his hands in a circle above his head.

"Once again, I don't need your lot tinkering with my plans!"

He unleashed the Sound Snatchers, which swarmed around the sails.

Amari aimed her glowing Orb at them. A purple flash erupted with a gust of wind, causing our boat to spin in a whirlpool again.

Gray continued dancing and prancing atop the Tower Clock and sang,

> *"What would you have expected of me?*
> *If not, to deal the sting?*
> *Play by the rules? I disagree!*
> *Now, give me everything!"*

Buzz and I flipped and flapped, trying to escape the Sound Snatchers.

Elena, Conall, and Lyle, swinging from ropes dangling from a Blue Whale above, landed on the deck in front of us and, pointing to Gray, sang out together—

> *"Who is this man who would scare us now?*
> *Shake the land and sea.*
> *Twist past and present into knots—"*

Amari joined in the chorus and added—

> *"Delete our history."*

Buzz and I joined in and together, sang out—

> *"We are the Folk who fell to earth.*
> *Wingless and confused."*

Conall and Elena replied—

> *"Silent thoughts corroding self,*
> *Cancelled and removed,"*

The storm raged. A Blue Whale surfaced. Gray cried out,

"I am the chosen, I claim the apex throne!"

My wing buds stung, and I shouted at him,

"We are the true believers! We imagine what could
be. Unknot the threads of hopefulness.
Renew our history."

The Gray, still dancing, shrieked—

"What would you have expected of me?
If not, to deal a sting? Play by the rules, I disagree.
Now, give me everything!
I am the chosen—"

Suddenly, a Blue Whale lifted its enormous body out of the river and, with its massive fin, swiped Gray into the swirling waters of the swollen Derwent River.

And he was gone.

CHAPTER 47
A SEA CHANGE

We watched the now-peaceful Derwent for signs of the Gray. The moonlight shimmered across its surface. There was a frost in the air.

"Where is he?" said Amari.

"Five fathoms down, I hope," replied Buzz.

"He didn't stand a chance against this current," said Conall.

Looking skyward, I held out my Lorifolk hand. "I think it's snowing!"

"That's curious," said Conall, gazing at the snow falling from the drab sky.

"The river, look!" said Elena. "It's beginning to freeze."

"The Derwent is freezing?" replied Conall. "That is remarkable."

Sound Snatchers harmlessly fell to the ground around us, like autumn Cherry Blossoms.

"He'll be trapped under this ice," said Amari.

"I guess so," said Buzz, sweeping the Sound Snatchers off the deck with his Lorifolk foot.

"I can't swim!" cried the Gray, as he surfaced, gasping for air.

We all ran to the port side and peered over the boat rail.

"I don't believe it," said Buzz.

"What should we do?" said Amari.

"We can't leave him!" cried Elena, reaching for an oar.

"Careful, Elena," said Conall. "It may be a trick."

The Gray slowly sank.

"He's gone under again," said Amari.

I heard a rumbling sound rolling up the river towards us. "Is that a tremor I can feel?"

Lyle turned to Amari and said, "Amari, the Vistoculos!" In an instant, he held it on his head and concentrated as the gears, cogs, and levers clicked and whirled, and each eyepiece swelled.

"He's below us, on a rock, five fathoms down. He's drowning. I can hear him—"

'Immerse me in, swish me about.
I can feel a change, I sense a doubt.
Sinking slowly, air bereft.
Has my endless rage, dissolved and left?
If I don't surface and sink below,
would it change the world?
Who would know?

Maybe good isn't so bad?
Lorifolk have it in the bag.
It really is a job to be, very angry endlessly.
From Gray to Simeon, but then not quite.
I'm now a shadow between black and white.

My plan, to be fair, was deeply flawed.

Wrong's on a scale that's very broad.
I get, my thinking, was ill-considered.
The earthquake was unintentionally triggered.
It's not as if I was unpredictable.
I created chaos, clearly visible.

From Gray to Simeon, but then not quite.
Malevolent to benevolent in one night?
A business model of whale oil shares.
Crashed when Lamplighters sold all theirs.

Then the war, well—I had a quota to meet.
And now I was getting back on my feet.
A musical quest, oh so sublime.
The prize to rule both space and time.
I had a choice, I jumped too soon.
Greed does that, and now, I'm doomed.

From Gray to Simeon, but then not quite.
I'm now a shadow between black and white.
I'm thinking, maybe go up for air?
Would a hand reach out?
I doubt they'd care.

Is pleasant but alive a better vow?
Than remaining mean but drowned from now?
And will my Cat know it's me,
without an evil vocabulary?

I've one last chance, a coda to my song.
I see the difference between right and wrong!
I have a choice, to live or die.
Simeon lives, I'll give that a try!'

There was a splash, and through a small hole in the ice, Gray surfaced, gasping for air.

"Help me, please!" he screamed.

"The port side," said Lyle as we quickly paced across the deck. Some of us climbed over the boat rail and warily stepped onto the thin ice just as the hole shut.

"No, he's gone again," said Buzz from the deck, ignoring the thumping sound from under the ice.

"Don't be absurd, Buzz," said Elena. "He's just below the ice."

Elena struck the ice with the oar and said, "I'm not going to let a living creature drown."

"I'll help too," said Conall, slipping his way across the ice to Elena.

"Buster," shouted Elena," I need your help—now!"

"Elena, just think for a moment," shouted Buzz.

I turned to Buzz, "What do we say, Buzz? All life is sacred!"

Buzz looked me in my Lorifolk eye, then watched us struggle to crack the ice with the oar. He climbed the rail, stepped onto the ice, stomped through it, and said,

"My Lorifolk blood tells me I'm going to regret this day."

The ice cracked open, Buzz reached into the freezing water, lifted the lifeless Gray out by his collar and dropped him onto the wet ice.

"Done!" said Buzz, wiping his hands on his coat.

The Lorikeets on the riverbank squawked.

Gray woke, gasped for air and spluttered, "Oh, thank you, thank you. Dear souls, thank you!"

Buzz, with a look of disgust, replied, "Stop your whining, Gray!"

"My name is Simeon," he coughed, rolling onto his side. "I've left the Gray on the riverbed."

"Oh, right," said Buzz. "And we're supposed to believe that?"

Conall knelt on the ice and helped Gray turn on his side, then looked up at Buzz and said, "Let him rest, Buzz."

"Rest? Don't you see? This—Simeon, Mr Gray, the Gray—whoever he is, caused the tremor that changed Blossom and me into—"

"Lorifolk, just like me," replied Amari.

"Yes, Lorifolk," said Buzz. "And now he's had this —underwater—"

"Epiphany?" added Elena.

"Whatever—" said Buzz, "And wants us to believe he's changed? Well, I'm not convinced!"

The ground around us shook, and the mast of the Acielle cracked.

"Quickly," said Lyle. "Move away from the mast."

"That was a very strong quake," said Conall.

The Gray coughed and spluttered, "I told you, resetting the Tempo Spirale has been impossible. It craves melody. I feed it what I collect from the Sound Snatchers, but it reacts with tremors and quakes."

"You know where the Tempo Spirale is?" asked Elena, kneeling on the ice beside him.

"Where is it?" demanded Lyle.

"Please tell us," begged Conall.

"It's complicated," pleaded Gray.

"Make it simple then," said Amari.

"Get on your feet," shouted Buzz, dragging Gray across the ice to the riverbank. "And show us, where it is!"

CHAPTER 48
THE LIBRARY AGAIN

Onré poured me a honey tea and offered ginger flakes from a silver tray with pictures of Dolphins and Seals. I thanked him and leaned back in the library chair. Vistarian Lyle, Amari, Elena, and Conall sat around an old wooden table with a large map laid out on it.

Vistarian Lyle ran his fingers over a line on the map and asked, "Are you sure the directions are correct?"

"That's what Simeon told Buzz," replied Conall, writing out directions from a brass compass.

"Simeon?" asked Vistarian Lyle.

"Simeon Gray," replied Elena, sipping her tea. "He's asked that we use his given name."

"He said he's spurned his evil ways," said Conall.

"Buzz isn't convinced," said Amari, reading the map. "And is watching him. It's only a half-day trek, south along the Derwent."

"I scanned the horizon earlier," said Vistarian Lyle. "It's fractured and very unstable. I'm not sure it's at all wise to follow a trail led by The Gray, it could be another trick."

"What choice do we have?" replied Conall. "He said he'd been trying to unlock the Tempo Spirale, to control time."

"But needed to solve a sonata," added Elena.

"A sonata?" said Vistarian Lyle. "You mean—?"

"As in a piece of music—sonata," replied Elena, placing her tea on the table. "With a start, middle, and an end."

"He said he was feeding the Tempo Spirale sounds," added Amari. "Captured by his Sound Snatchers."

"Composing my operetta has certainly been a puzzle to me," said Elena, with a smile.

"How so, my love?" asked Conall.

"Well, the melody of a sonata is like a quest. The start is the journey, the middle gets all exciting and the finale, everything's resolved—"

"Solved, if the right melody was played to it?" added Conall.

"Yes, but a melody could have infinite variations," replied Elena.

"Not exactly," said Conall, deep in thought. "There are only five thousand and forty possible variations to a seven-note melody."

"Most impressive," said Onré. "More tea, Amari?"

Conall continued. "Of course, that's only if one used all seven notes of the musical scale, C, D, E, F, G, A and B—and no sharps or repetition."

"Naturally," added Onré. "More tea?"

"How long would it take to play that many variations?" asked Vistarian Lyle.

"And what if the Tempo Spirale doesn't like the melody?" asked Amari. "The Gray—Simeon, said it's causing tremors and quakes."

"Well, first," said Elena. "Let's find this place where Simeon says it is—"

Simeon entered the library. His hands were tied. Buzz was close behind.

"Assuming," said Buzz, giving Simeon a push. "We're not being led on a wild Human Folk chase."

"We've few choices, Buzz," said Elena. "And these are not necessary," she added, untying Simeon's hands.

I once saw a Raven tied by its legs to a farmer's fence. It was a warning to other Birds not to eat the apricots in the trees. Seeing a creature's hands tied, even Simeon's, made me sad. I quietly stepped out of the library into the corridor.

"Blossom," said Elena. "Are you ready for a walk to—"

"Buzz, wasn't Blossom with you?"

"No," replied Buzz.

I listened a little longer, peeking through the door.

"Amari," said Vistarian Lyle, "Please go find Blossom."

I quickly made my way down the corridor before Amari could catch up to me.

CHAPTER 49
UNDER THE CHERRY BLOSSOM TREE

A s I sat under the cherry blossom tree growing near the front steps of the Tower, its pink and white branches swayed in the gentle wind. Amari arrived a moment later.

"Blossom? We were wondering where you were."

"I'm just problem-solving, that's all," I replied.

"Ah, and have you solved the problem?"

"Not really. When I was a Lorikeet, if I needed to think hard about something, I'd fly high above the trees, and glide with the wind, and it would whisper to me. It seemed to make the problem—"

"Less of a problem?" replied Amari, sitting down beside me.

"Yes."

"Can I help, Blossom?"

"Yesterday, when we were walking about the valley, I asked Buzz, 'If you could snap your Lorifolk fingers and change back into a Lorikeet, would you?'"

"And what did he say?"

"He said to me, 'What a silly question.' And walked on ahead of me."

"Oh, I see," said Amari.

"And what would you do?"

I turned to Amari and snapped my Lorifolk fingers.

"Nothing happens."

"I'm sorry, Blossom."

"Thanks anyway for listening."

Amari stood.

"The Vistarian has asked us to follow Simeon Gray to a point about a half-day walk south of here, to seek and unlock the Tempo Spirale."

"Sounds like a plan," I said, getting to my Lorifolk feet.

Buzz arrived wearing a backpack, swinging a second one in his hand.

"Catch!" he shouted to me.

I caught it, just as Elena, Conall and Vistarian Lyle arrived, carrying smaller packs.

"Good catch!" said Simeon, following behind. He kind of smiled at me.

"Oh, thanks," I said, putting it on, unsure of what else to say.

"Ready for a long walk, Blossom?" Elena asked.

A rumbling sound echoed up the valley from the south. Lyle threw on his pack and said,

"We need to leave at once."

CHAPTER 50

THE ORGANON

We followed Simeon for a long time along a steep mountain trail and arrived at a rock wall of blue and gold columns reaching to the clouds. In its middle, the columns twisted and curved into an archway, covered with odd shapes, like those on the Vistoculos.

Under the arch, a path led to steps carved deep into the rock. As Simeon rested under the archway, Conall pointed to the strange shapes above him.

"You're a smart man, Mr Finlay. What do they say?" said Simeon.

"It's Professor, actually—and that one there is the symbol for infinity."

"Watch, Professor," said Simeon.

"I'm watching," said Conall.

"No, take out your pocket watch, please, Professor."

Buzz turned to Simeon.

"I hope this is not some kind of game, Gray?"

"It's not."

He turned to Conall.

"On my say, repeat a seven-count, twenty-one times. One, two, three, four—"

"—Five, six, seven. A seven-count, twenty-one times, I understand," said Conall.

"Vistarian, when the counting starts, you and Amari need to wave the Orb—tracing the pattern of the infinity symbol."

"And what can the rest of us do?" asked Elena.

"A Chicken dance, maybe?" sneered Buzz.

"Warm your hands, Elena. Blossom, Buster, stand back."

My wing buds tingled.

"Did you say, warm your hands?" replied Elena.

"The keys will be cold," said Simeon.

"Keys?" said Elena.

"Trust me," said Simeon.

Buzz gave a heavy sigh and said, "Oh, you have got—"

"We trust you," said Elena.

"Ready, everyone?" he said, holding up his hand. "Professor Finlay, on my mark—"

"Now!"

Conall looked at his stopwatch and began.

> *"One, two, three, four, five, six, seven—One, two, three, four, five, six, seven—"*

Simeon nodded to Lyle and Amari, who, with both hands on the Orb, waved it in the infinity pattern over the symbols. Conall continued his seven-count.

> *"One, two, three, four, five, six, seven—One, two, three, four, five, six, seven—"*

With his hands, Simeon echoed the movement of the Orb. The symbols over the arch glowed, and the columns shook.

> *"One, two, three, four, five, six, seven—One, two, three, four, five, six, seven—"*

From under the arch, a low, wide shape emerged from within the rock and grew into a broad maple-wood box. Wind rushed from pipes growing out of its top, and a mist lifted to reveal black and white keys.

"An Organon," said Conall. "A pipe organ!"

"Don't stop counting," said Simeon.

Conall continued.

> *"—two, three, four, five, six, seven—One, two, three, four, five, six, seven—"*

A marble seat emerged from its base, and Simeon waved to Elena to come.

"Slowly now, be seated," he said.

Elena looked scared.

> *"One, two, three, four, five, six, seven—One, two, three, four, five, six, seven—"*

"Gray, are you sure about this?" said Conall.

"Don't stop counting," shouted Simeon.

Conall continued.

> *"One, two, three, four, five, six, seven—One, two, three, four, five, six, seven—"*

"Amari, keep the Orb ready," said Lyle.

Amari stood, strong and straight, her hands clenched to the Orb. Buzz stood beside her. "I'm with you," he said, his hands on the glowing Orb, beside hers.

> *"One, two, three, four, five, six, seven—One, two,*
> *three, four, five, six, seven—"*

Elena warmed her hands and cautiously sat on the marble seat, the symbols twinkling.

"So, what should I play?"

> *"One, two, three, four, five, six, seven—One, two,*
> *three, four, five, six, seven—"*

Simeon pulled from his coat a stack of pages with lines and symbols on them and placed it on a stand above the keys.

"This musical score was written after many sleepwalks. Play, light and gentle. Use all seven notes of the musical scale."

> *"One, two, three, four, five, six, seven—One, two,*
> *three, four, five, six, seven—"*

Elena placed her fingers on the keys, then quickly snapped her hands back and blew on them to warm them.

"They are cold!" she said.

"Light and gentle, dear lady," said Simeon.

> *"One, two, three, four, five, six, seven—One, two,*
> *three, four, five, six, seven—"*

Elena began to play the seven notes of the musical scale, C, D, E, F, G, A and B.

The symbols twinkled.

"One, two, three, four, five, six, seven—"

Elena then played a beautiful melody that became a gentle, flowing stream of sound.

"Excellent," said Simeon, turning the page of music. "Now for a minor variation."

Elena played the variation. A candlestick and stops emerged from the Organon, and it began to shake. The trees around us began to vibrate, and I felt unsteady on these Lori-folk feet.

"If a minor variation is causing this shaking," said Amari. "We wouldn't want to hear—"

"Now for a major variation, if you would please, dear lady," said Simeon, his hand waving in time to the melody.

Elena played the variation. Clouds of dense fog blew from its pipes. The shaking around us grew.

"Not good," said Buzz.

"Gray—ah—Simeon," said Lyle. "I sense a quake is near. Can we hurry along?"

"Look—" I said. "The pipes." Snowflakes emerged from the pipes, dancing in the air to the music, before gently falling to the ground and melting.

"Professor, you said there are how many variations to a seven-note melody?"

"Five thousand and forty."

"Play, dear lady. The notation now says, 'Vivace!'"

Elena played lively and fast. Sound blasted from the pipes, and all around us shook.

"My hands," cried Elena. "I can't, I can't stop—"

Elena tried to free her hands, but they seemed to be bound to the keys.

A candlestick fell.

"Play, play," shouted Simeon over the melody. "It says, 'Presto!'"

Elena, in a kind of trance, played even more quickly. Everywhere around us shook uncontrollably. Conall and I fell to the ground.

"Gray," cried Conall. "Her hands—"

"Not now, Professor," said Simeon, turning the page. "Play! It says, 'Prestissimo!'"

Elena, still dazed, played the melody extremely fast. All kinds of Birds swooped and screeched above us.

"Prestissimo! Prestissimo!" demanded Simeon.

The sky turned to night, and stars spun around us in a blur. Elena continued to play.

"Look! The moon and stars!" I cried.

"Prestissimo! Prestissimo!"

The middle column cracked. A blinding light shone. Faces of Lamplighters, soldiers, the crew of the Aurora, Blue Whales, Seals and Royal Penguins appeared through the light.

"It's working!" said Simeon, "It's unlocking —'Prestissimo!'"

"I can't keep playing—" said Elena, exhausted. "I must rest—"

"Elena!" cried Conall, rushing to help her.

The music stopped.

A rumble, at the very same tempo, replaced it. The sky seemed to close in on us, and the crack in the column slowly closed. The beam of blinding light almost faded away.

"No, no, it can't be," said Simeon, hitting the keys. "The keys, they are frozen—"

A booming bass rumble quickened.

"Sing everybody," mumbled Elena. "Sing the melody!"

We tried to sing, but our voices were drowned out by the

booming bass. The crack in the column continued to close. We all trembled.

"It's not working!" cried Amari.

"Blossom," shouted Lyle. "The whistle around your neck!"

I felt for the whistle around my neck and blew its B note as loudly as I possibly could. The crack in the column shuddered, and the infinity symbol on the arch shone brightly.

"And I'll play my D whistle!" Lyle blew his D for Dalzell whistle, then pulled a whistle from his pack and tossed it to Amari.

"Amari, catch," he said. "It's the A note. Blow it now!"

Amari blew the A whistle. The crack shuddered again.

"I'm in!" cried Buzz. He blew the F whistle.

"Me too," said Conall, then he blew the C whistle.

The crack shuddered.

Elena blew the E whistle, and the crack stopped. The rumble slowed to a steady heartbeat.

"Lyle," said Elena. "The G note, the G note must be played!"

Lyle pulled the G whistle from his pack and threw it at Simeon, but it fell short—Buzz caught it.

"Gray?" said Buzz.

"Yes?"

"This G note is yours, I believe—"

Buzz placed it around his neck and, smiling, said,

"Simeon."

"Thank you, Buzz," said Simeon, and turning to us all, cried out,

"Everyone on my count—"

He pointed to each of us in turn, and we blew our whistles. C for Conall, D for Lyle Dalzell, E for Elena, F for Friend, that's Buzz, G for Gray, A for Amari and B for me.

"And now," said Simeon. "Together in harmony—"

We all played the melody together, and it was beautiful, and the crack in the column opened, and a glowing light poured out and warmed us.

And the rumble became a gentle heartbeat, and the sky began to clear, and time was unlocked, released to play a chorus of hope.

CHAPTER 51

THE PROMISE

T he sun's morning rays peaked through the cherry blossom branches and shone upon Elena and Conall as they stood side-by-side in the green fields of the Tower Gardens. Vistarian Lyle held a crystal orb of blue water over their hands. Amari, Buzz and I stood behind, holding water mirrors that reflected the quiet blue sky. Conall and Elena then said aloud,

> *"What is love? I feel your heartbeat.*
> *What is love? I sense your ache.*
> *What is love?*
> *We roam its course, without destination."*

Elena then washed Conall's hands in the flowing water and said,

> *"Conall, the river's course is ever-changing, but it*
> *carries us. Today, I make my seven-year*
> *promise to you."*

Conall then washed Elena's hands and said,

> *"Elena, we may struggle in its current, but will surf*
> *in its wake. Today, I make my seven-year*
> *promise to you."*

Lyle poured the water over their held hands and said,

> *"The river's tide will forever be a friend.*
> *Its ebb and its flood forever will flow."*

The Lorikeets called, and the cherry blossoms danced about them.

Lyle placed his hands below theirs, and Buzz, Amari and I placed our Lorifolk hands on top.

And together we said,

"Let it be known!"

And we all hugged and cheered.

CHAPTER 52
THE VISTARIAN'S DINING ROOM

O nré poured Elena a tall glass of cherry wine.

"Cherry wine, Onré, how did—?"

"The Tower walls have ears, Elena," he said, winking at me.

Conall raised his glass. "Here's to Onré."

"Which I second," said Vistarian Lyle.

"Ah, someone is here," said Onré, opening the dining room door.

Elena tapped Conall on the hand and said, "No toasts yet, my love; we're not all here."

Simeon entered carrying his Cat and a bottle of wine. Lyle stood to greet him.

"I hope you don't mind, Vistarian. Snuffles doesn't like being left alone."

"Snuffles is—lovely," I said, not too convincingly. "But not too close to me. I have a—strange relationship with Cats."

"Of course," said Simeon. "A Lorifolk thing?"

"More, a Rainbow Lorikeet thing," I replied.

Elena stood, pulled out a chair and said, "Simeon, come, sit near Conall and me."

Amari bounced into the room with Buzz and, flopping into a chair, reached for a drink.

"Buzz is very testing!" she said.

"I could have told you that, Amari," I said.

Buzz poured two glasses of bubbly-blue water and gave one to Amari.

"I'm just competitive, that's all. I was clearly first to the summit of the Blue Hill."

"Clearly?" said Amari.

"And from whose point of view would that clearly be?" said Lyle.

Buzz grinned, "Me, a Lorifolk."

Elena stood and said,

> *"Friendships have no borders,*
> *Friendships have no bounds."*

Then Conall, Lyle, Buzz, and I stood and replied,

> *"Friends, come back tomorrow,*
> *Friends are all around."*

And Vistarian Lyle, Amari, Simeon and Onré stood alongside us, and together we said,

> *"Friendships have no borders.*
> *Friendships have no bounds.*
> *Friends come back tomorrow.*
> *Friends are all around."*

CHAPTER 53

THE STAIRWAY AWAY

With our packs on our backs, we gathered in the gold and blue glow of the Stairway Away, as the evening sunlight shone on the Organ Pipes of this remarkable world. Amari and Vistarian Lyle watched as the Lorikeets chatted and called in the distance.

"Professor Finlay," said Simeon. "Here is the letter we discussed."

Conall placed his pack on the ground, took the letter, and, shaking Simeon's hand, said, "I'm very appreciative, Simeon, thank you."

"Believe it or not, I still have some influence with the Institute Directors. Now that the war is over, they'll see the wisdom in your hydroelectric scheme. Your geological mapping of the Great Lake is excellent."

"I'm confident it has the capacity of seven megawatts!"

"I'm sure it will. Safe travels! Say hello to Hobart from me."

"No regrets?" said Conall.

"My time is best served here," said Simeon. "Remember, as

soon as you enter the stairway, the wind will take you; no time for waving goodbye."

He gave a polite bow to Conall.

"Goodbye, Simeon Gray," said Elena, shaking his hand.

"Goodbye, Elena Meijer. You've time now to complete the final act of that operetta."

"That's very true, and looking around me, I have ample inspiration!"

"Your friends saved your voice from my Sound Snatchers. I will forever be in debt to you for the kindness you have shown to me, a lost soul."

"Something lost is only so until found. Goodbye, Simeon."

"You have written an operetta, Elena?" asked Amari.

"It is wonderful," I added. "It's called 'Latente' and is —amazing!"

"It's a work in progress, Amari, just like your apprentice-ship." She pointed to Lyle. "He is a good man; listen to him."

"I have much to do here; the Florna need me," said Amari.

"As you need them. Goodbye, Amari," said Elena.

Conall placed his pack on his shoulder and took out his pocket watch. "Are we on time to make this tidal wind, Vistarian Lyle?"

"Unless the moon has other plans, Conall, you'll fly on this tide."

"I salute you, Vistarian Lyle," said Conall.

"Time starts again, Time Tinker, and one day, the Spirits willing, we will meet again."

"Now, give me a hug, Conall!" said Lyle.

Amari then gave Buzz and me a big hug. "My investiture is less than one of your years away."

"I'll be here," said Buzz.

"Promise?" said Amari.

"Promise!" said Buzz as he felt the A whistle around his neck.

"Amari, Conall has a gift for you," I said.

Conall gave his pocket watch to Amari. "Remember to wind it each day, it keeps excellent time."

"To remind you of all of us," I said.

Onré whispered to Vistarian Lyle, "Sir, it's time."

Lyle coughed and placed a hand on Buzz's shoulder. "Time to say our goodbyes."

"Why? Is someone leaving?" said Buzz, wiping the tears from his Lorifolk eyes.

Lyle wiped away his tears and said,

"Cheeky, from the very first day we met. There you were, stealing apples on the docks."

"You wanted a second set of eyes."

"You gave me that Buster and so much more. I'm forever grateful."

"I salute you, Vistarian."

"Remember," said Simeon. "As you enter the stairway, the wind will take you."

"Farewell, friends," said Amari.

"Goodbye!" we said.

Buzz, Elena, Conall, and I stood in the gold and blue glow of the Stairway Away, waving our final farewell to our new friends and an old one.

And as we stepped through its entrance, the evening sunlight slipped away, and the chatter of the Lorikeets faded.

CHAPTER 54

ELIZABETH STREET, HOBART

A little Human Folk waved a hat and cried—

"World War is Over, Armistice Terms Accepted!
Hostilities Cease on all Fronts!"

The Hobart steam train shrieked, the bells of the Clock Tower rang, and the Human Folk chit-chatted and surrounded us, pushing Buzz and me slowly along the Salamanca docks towards Battery Point.

Above the hullabaloo, Buzz shouted,

"I will always remember you, Blossom, always."

But I lost him in the crowd of Human Folk.

Then he reappeared and looked back, beaming.

"I will always remember—"

"I love you, Buzz!" I called to him. "I will always remember."

Then, he was gone, a Lorifolk lost in the surging crowd of Human Folk.

"Friends to the end of time," I thought to myself.

I turned south and looked out over the Derwent to the horizon. The crowd's celebrations had faded like the purple and pink sky. My wing buds tingled. I took a deep breath and smiled.

'A second in time, a drop of rain.
A fleeting smile, a moment's pain.

To the end of time, I will be yours,
to the end of time.

Weightless is our love, below us and above.
Floating in my heart, filling me within.

Taking me so high. Across our gentle sky.
Connecting all our days, the months, the years, the
ways.

Weightless is our love, below us and above.
To the end of time.
The end of time.'

I began to run, and as my pace quickened, I smiled as joyous memories flashed by in an instant, and in a flip and a flap, I launched myself off the cliff edge, arms outstretched and felt my wings.

Just like a Rainbow Lorikeet.

THE ~~END~~ START

THE CURTAIN CALL

'Time is a concept hard to explain,
to start at the start, we go around again.
Where is the start, near the end,
and that's confusing, as time can bend.

Tick, tock, halt, depart.
Before you arrive, remember to start.

Bending time is a curious thing.
To consider what the future will bring.
Because that's at the start, not at the end.
Which passed the past and came back again.

Tock, tick, proceed, delay.
Look ahead to the past, while you're away.

So, to start at the start, we go back to the end.
Where our story begins, but also ends.
To tinker with time, we turn back a page.

And visit your past, my post-industrial age.

Tick, tock, halt, depart.
Before you arrive, remember to start.

A sailing ship, a Bird by two,
a singer, geologist, captain and crew.
Where the wise may be wrong and answers few,
depending on your point of view.

Tock, tick, proceed, delay.
Look ahead to the past, while you're away.

Time is a concept I've already explained,
ends at the start and comes back again.
There at the start, you'll find the end,
curling around a spiral bend.

Tick, tock, halt, depart.
Before you arrive, remember to start!

To sing a song I sang before.
To sail the waves that left a shore.
To find a place I've already been.
To fly upside down.
To live a dream!'

ABOUT THE AUTHOR

Michael Collins is a singer-songwriter and librettist. He wrote the Blossom and Buzz Musical Trilogy between 2020 and 2024 as Vincent Michaels and is collaborating with amazing composers on the music. To listen to Blossom's songs, visit lorifolk.com

Antarctica is a recurring location in Michael's stories. SAEF, Securing Antarctica's Environmental Future, is an amazing group of researchers exploring ways to protect the future of Antarctica and our planet. Knowledge is like a time machine, unlocking the past, present and future, and you can help change the future. To find out more, visit arcsaef.com

www.ingramcontent.com/pod-product-compliance
Lightning Source LLC
Chambersburg PA
CBHW021009180626
46814CB00003B/1210